I0588518

Ani's Portrait

My String Bag Back Home

Julie Mota Kondi

Copyright © Julie Mota Kondi 2024
All rights reserved. No part of this book may be reproduced or transmitted in any form
or by any means, electronic or mechanical, including photocopying, recording or by any
information storage and retrieval system, without prior written permission of the Publisher
below. The Australian Copyright Act 1968 allows one chapter only, or 10% of this book,
whichever is the greater, to be photocopied by any educational institution for its educational
purposes provided that the educational institution (or body that administers it) has given a

copyright notice to the Copyright Agency (Australia) under the Act.

Paperback ISBN: 978-0-6459322-8-7

First Published in 2024 by

**First Nations Writers Festival International Limited
T/as First Nations Publishers**

A Registered Charity (ABN 79 655 932 979)

2/53 Junction St, Nowra NSW 2540, Australia
Phone: +61 491 851 353
Email: firstnationswritersfestival@gmail.com
Web: www.firstnationswritersfestival.org

FB: www.facebook.com/firstnationswritersfestival.com

Cover Design: Busybird Publishing
Cover Photo: Julie Mota Kondi
Typeset: Busybird Publishing
Line Edited: Anna Borzi AM 2024

Printed and bound in Australia by IngramSpark

This Book is a work of fiction. Names, characters, places and incidents are either a
product of the author's imagination or are used fictitiously. Any resemblance to actual people
living or dead, events or locales, is entirely co-incidental.

In Loving Memory of Emil Tangole

(2003-2024)

Balogu!

I look up at the coconut trees,
I look up to see you there.
No more Kuku nonghi nonghi
Balogu!

One week today.
Why did you run?
I was coming on Monday.
Balogu!

Now the kokomos are gone.
Only silence fills the forest paths.
You only notice your little brother's broken grief and your sister's tears
drenched in despair.
Balogu!

Memories of our family's happy moments haunt us now. Remember
how we used to fly in the first-class seats to Port Moresby.
We ate also in the busy restaurants in the city.
You lived in that privileged life.
Balogu!

Now your departure from this life haunts me.
Where did your Kaku and I go wrong?
Balogu!

Now I wait for the sunset to hide my grief
My tears will never run dry.
Why?
Balogu!

Now the silence in the house hits me hard.
Goodbyes are never easy passages in life.

For Lolote, Waiyora, Taroa and Lebo Koi

Thank you

My husband Bernard, and children Annlyn, Andrew and Marian

Major Anthony Mota and Family

Elders and relatives at Kawutu Wakore village Ruango;
and First Nations Writers Festival for publishing this story.

Contents

Part 1

Na Vironu Sedo, dubo kotise anumbirena.
(I recall with fondness the memories as I ponder with a reflective gaze).

Part 2

Sorara Da Kiki Saida Erena (Micro Perspectives of Identity)

Part 3
The Gelus [Micro Politics of Belonging]

Persona Dramatis

Immediate Family

Mama- main character
Mother to Dubo/ Caitlin, Mila Kaiymei and Dido

Wife to Papa

Daughter to Avia Agira.

A retired public servant who is living in her husband's village and as a migrant settler tries to make her place in society as a Mother.

Caitlin whose traditional name is Dubo
Mama's and Papa's eldest daughter, eldest sister to Mila, Dido and Kaiymei She is studying at university and it is to whom these stories are being sent.

Mila
Second daughter to Mama and Papa, younger sister of Dubo/Caitlin, and elder sister to Dido and Kaiymei. Mila is in high school and emails family correspondence to her sister, Caitlin. A young adult in a diaspora cosmopolitan village lifestyle.

Avia Agira
Mother to Mama, grandmother to Dubo/Caitlin, Mila, Dido and Kaiymei and Mother-in-law to Papa. Retired school teacher in her sixties. She relates her diaspora migrant identity to her children with nostalgia and reminiscing encounters.

Kaiymei
The youngest child, sister, daughter and grandchild in the family. In prep school, an extrovert person who is hardly indoors.

Dido

A teenager, only son to Mama and Papa, grandson to Avia Agira and only brother to Caitlin, Mila and Kaiymei. Lives in the village haus boi awaiting his initiation custom ceremony.

Papa

Father to Caitlin, Mila, Kaiymei, and Dido.

Married to Mama and son-in-law to Avia Agira.

He is often in the family plantation estate and has less contact with emails or family communications to Caitlin.

The Antagonists

Tamana Gelu

Papa's youngest brother, an early childhood teacher in the village. In his mid-thirties, married to Kina Gelu and has three kids. He is the family's main Antagonist with his wife. He often behaves in erratic psychopathic ways and has a very violent temper.

Kina Gelu

She is a house wife married to Tamana Gelu and is jealous of the Dubo family achievements. A gambler and drunkard she has a loud mouth attitude in all her dealings. She is one of the family Antagonists

Watermelon

Known in the neighbourhood as the village gossip, she lives next to the Gelus' as well and is the main instigator of community brawls. However, she is the community worship leader for prayer meetings. She is married with school age children and takes part in all women group activities.

Back Page

She is Papa's youngest sister who is challenging Papa over the family inheritance and estate ownership.

Rambo

A cousin of Papa who preys on Papa at the main family estate block. Papa had taken him to court but he continues to try to assassinate Papa.

Sister Mamo

Watermelon's daughter who babysits Kaiymei when Dubo and Mila are not around. She is the same age as Mila and is of quiet temperament.

The Writer's Statement

This is a semi-autobiographical work of which the characters are fictionalised as are some places in the story. If there are any resemblances to anyone it is pure coincidence. This is a work of fiction based on actual events and oral history of the Bebeli tribe of West New Britain Province, at Ruango village. An alternate history.

There are at least three story telling processes that are employed to develop the story's plot. These construction processes are adapted from the Korafe Mokorua; language group dialects, of the Binandere group of languages from Northern Province, Papua New Guinea.

For many generations in our indigenous society our people, the Korafe Mokorua, have held our traditional folklores, legends and oral history as valuable materials of worth within our domestic spaces. Whether public, engendered or intimate and sacred. Especially since the art of storytelling is an important form of bonding and maintaining one's cultural identity in our traditional society. More often, it attaches the indigenous people to their ancestral lands and the physical surrounding landscapes, landmarks and social spaces.

We believe that anyone can tell a story but there are some people who are exceptionally gifted story tellers. They are talented, and skilled, to tell a story that engages the attention of audiences' imaginations with compelling topics and colourful insight into human nature.

Through their own imagined spaces for each of these stories, the narrator introduces the story and formats to be used. Whether it shall be sung or orated or performed in interactive skits and dance drama.

In every act of public speaking the narrator always starts by using the phrase, *"Na geka eini saida erena."*

This is literally to excuse the audience, so as to make a statement or an oral presentation. It is only after this phrase is used that the narrator continues on with the presentation. This is more like general manners, or courtesy, for public speaking within and among the Korafe Mokorua language speaking indigenous tribes.

In many instances, and in a manner of social values, this act within public speaking is a form of an indigenous traditional and intellectual humility when public speaking.

While like a "Gasegha", Narrative Poetry is a commonly known public Korafe Mokorua traditional poetry recital, the story telling process is an act of Performative Poetic acts that are usually sung in home coming introductions after a long absence. They are made by women elders of the person.

However, in this particular instance this novel introduces Caitlin, the main character and her filial ties to her wider network of family relations both immediate and extended. In so doing, it untangles the diaspora impact of inter marriage families' lingual issues in modern Papua New Guinea. Whilst, in many instances, unpacking identity values of belonging and place-making in a multi ethnic / cultural environment and the rich tapestry of experiences held within those linking networks.

In other words, it is very much a literary portrayal of how change evolves and affects our daily communication within.

The novel as social narrative uses active memory as a device to introduce concepts of changing social landscapes and its impact on identity values. To that extent it redirects the lens of lived experiences to the indigene person. A mother and daughter relationship journal of interactions with others in the community. In hindsight it engages a dialogue on French Philosopher, Paul Ricouer's theoretical work on the concept of memory, forgetfulness and collective memories in literature. Here I present concept notes on this narrative experience as recorded in this novel exegesis.

The Idea Behind having short concept note themes is from the Korafe Mokorua story telling traditional indigenous practice of the term referred to in the following Korafe Mokorua phrase, *"na Kiki saida erena among Nanda susumo emo ri."*

Translated this phrase would be: *the plot's main thematic concepts are hereby presented as a guide for readers.*

The whole project was an experimental work exploring the Korafe Mokorua narrative culture in a written format. However, the setting of the story is in West New Britain Province on the island of New Britain.

While our education system wants our stories to be in English and to use their narrative style our voices drown and disappear in the cultural ocean of ignorance.

In writing this project I hope that our way of telling our story can be respected and appreciated in the country.

Scene /Setting

I set the scene in West New Britain Province in an imagined village of the indigenous Bebeli speaking people. I also included references to cultural materials and references to episodic historical events through their people's lens to present a social narrative of the place and its people. This is to show how urban developments over time impact indigenous peoples' lifestyle choices and identity values.

I adopt the protest writing style of contemporary Papua New Guinea modern literature period of the nineteen sixties. Using the dissident voice of the indigene person in a changing evolving environment. I am interested in expanding the conversation of our nation's pre independence writers when they started writing about the consciousness of change on indigenous lives and lifestyle choices.

From Norah Vagi Brash satirical tone, to Kamalau Tawali's confrontational outbursts in modern verse, all are used here - in the description of the traditional Reiki dance for example. And saddled onto the story line I try to create a self-conscious awareness of the social landscapes of change.

However, it is Russell Soaba's poem *"To Follow the Rainbow"* [1967] that forms the basis of this narrative experience of the indigene person. Whilst the tone then was from the singular or dual lingual background and a first-generation migrant lens, this work in contrast introduces the modern diaspora1 person detached from their original village. At the same time, it reframes the concept of village setting or settlement communities in our modern urban village in Papua New Guinea and the multi lingual diaspora migrant experience into the literary.

In this particular story I am using the village setting in the New Guinea Islands region of Papua New Guinea. More specifically, on New Britain island. Here is a brief background of the place.

New Britain Island

The island was discovered by the western world and recorded in the 1500s by Portuguese explorers. It became an historic maritime transit port for the Pacific routes of early European whaling expeditions in the fifteenth and sixteenth century. Around when the Spice trade route transit ports to the Spice Islands was documented.

Today it remains an important site of Pacific colonisation by European Imperial governments; and became the human labour trade route from the Pacific to Europe 2. In the later part of the nineteen century the island became the Pacific colonial headquarters for the Imperial German government colonies in the Pacific. It was a strategic military maritime and air space in the Pacific theatre military history during the

---

1   There are nearly 3,000 languages in the Greater Pacific; of which nearly 1,000 belong to the nation of #PNG. ~1,000 languages [not including dialects], means at least 1,000 different cultures. When a marriage occurs, the wife often travels from her village to that of the husband, that is-migrates, without any prior knowledge of language or culture or social mores. This is possibly the greatest diaspora of multi lingual peoples in the world. Ed.

2   Indentured slavery. Ed.

two world wars and remains today an important historical landscape in the Pacific Islands region maritime economy.

In the context of modern history, the island's colonial past: from its plantation settlement history with the indigenous people of Bebeli, the social emancipation from the rich tapestry connecting the local people with their landscape, and the disruption of their way of life as a result of the invasion and intrusion of outsiders on their landscapes; requires a meticulous inquiry.

From black-birding expeditions to the Pacific theatre of war during the subsequent world wars and colonisation until national independence, hegemonic values have changed dramatically and sporadically. The random atrocities on indigenous lives and the destruction of communities by colonisers in episodes such as in nuclear testing, mining and the resettlement of indigenous communities from their traditional homelands, all remain part of our other Pacific Islands neighbour's dark heritage for those on New Britain island.

The impregnated silence of unspoken atrocities hover over our people's lives in cultural memories. In our modern literature in the country, the lived experiences of our local people here on New Britain Island are not often written nor talked about. Evan more so, where indigenous people like the Bebeli are marginalised and constantly pushed towards erasure of identity. Which persists even today.

The on-going power struggles between the colonised and the colonisers' justification for action, reactions and long-term significance, affect the historical narratives.

Creating a collective societal dependency on the notion of **master knows best** in turn further demonstrates to a wider extent our country's formal history through the lens of the coloniser.

Using that lens , we accept the Dimdim's version of how to tell our stories and in the process suppress the creative expressions, aspirations of our people and inherent memories of what happened within their own lens. Over millennia.

In this work, Ani's Portrait: The String Bag Back Home – the trailer is a metaphor for emotional baggage that is of cultural weight. It responds to the effect, and in turn subscribes to, one's values and ideologies of belonging and place making in Papua New Guinea.

Exegesis

The plot is constructed in three narrative development stages of intellectual Awakenings of the main character: Caitlin's mother [Mama]. From nostalgia to shame and individual insight of self-pity, the emotional ride engages in personal dialogues and self-consciousness of others reactions to her upon her interactions with them.

In the initial process the conceptual theme is based on the phrase *"Na Vironu sedo dubo kotise resena"* which literally translated would be *"as to remember with fondness as in contemplatio*n of *a memory or recollection of past events,"* or more aptly describing the personal reflective consciousness of the past through memories with bitter sweet emotions in the act of nostalgia (to be carried away by the reflective lens the socio-political landscapes of emotional energy exude).

On the other hand, the act of reminisce so overwhelmingly revisits the memory-scape with an enlightenment of time and experiences to our own prejudices and biases.

In the next stage I work around the thematic phrase, *"Na sorara geka eini saida* erena*"* which literally means when translated, *"Let it be known that I wish to make a point about jealousy or the acts of it"*.

It unpacks a series of incidents that are subtle yet distinct human behavioral emotions.

While in the final stage of this narrative, the thematic phrase is *"eresaka"*. It means *"so you say"* as a form of sarcasm. Thereby, to produce a satire. So, the devices that are used are from nostalgia and reminiscence with emotional enlightenment about socio cultural landscapes micro political struggles, a micro perspective lens on how change affects human relationships and its consequences over time. The literary tool here is how memory constructs and deconstructs social identity, including values, and its impacts on the local narratives.

The underlying motive is to show how memory is not only an active form of experience but an intimate intruder in time and space dynamics revisited. Here it retains an active form of making one's personal space relevant in connection to and in attesting to the diverging contested spaces in the story.

Using the female lens from a mother and daughter relationship, I want to discuss how human language within different interest peer groups and inter-generational levels in society view change from their own layers of cultural perspectives. As a consequence, unpacking the evolving micro perspectives of our village, and the micro politics of the cosmopolitan village lifestyle.

The story reverts from one peer group to another and from the main characters centralised version of events. In doing so, in many instances it challenges the social status quo and norms about women's status and roles in society but on a broader worldview, reflects the Melanesian society under change. Not abrupt and eruptive but gradual and in a reactive stance towards the evolving tide of influences.

The Idea Behind the Story

My daughter Dubo and I had these ongoing conversations about our dying cultures. The way values are compromised by people to serve justification of their actions, prejudices and vanity over the moral good of everyone, the community.

So, when I state the idea in writing this novel is an experimental work, it is an 'explorative exercise in literature'. My project for you. I am interested in adopting the critical race theory of which the Melanesian identity within literary culture re-visits my own traditional indigenous spiritual values of *place making*. Rendering the social values of storytelling by using nostalgia as a device of memory.

For story tellers like myself, who are women living in these times, it is very much a personal structure for cultural expression of identity for validation, on belonging and making a place in society, asserting and maintaining the status quo. To express the personal voice in literary space: the joys to be alive, young and ambitious. It becomes an arc of intellectual affirmation, acknowledging my indigeneity, status quo and racial orientation as a person and a writer within my own socio-political environment. You know what I mean?

I wanna adopt and apply micro political perspectives of how land grabbing exists and persist within our cultural lens in our local villages in the New Guinea Islands. Telling our stories through our own lens, you know what I mean? I ask this question in between the huge bites of my favourite cheese, flavoured snax brand biscuits and taking sips from my hot steaming locally brewed Goroka coffee.[3]

We are in the morning rush hours of weekend errands and family grocery runs when this conversation pops up again.

---

3 All colonial introductions. Ed.

This is where my daughter Dubo and I get to talk about stuff like the erasure of identity in land grabbing policies within our current state institutions; and policies that create bipolarity in binary blindness among our local people. This in turn triggers societal conflicts from disputes that increase law and order challenges in civil unrest incidents.

The undercurrents within the social narrative using the epistemology of coloured talk [re]visits, [re]frames and [re]imagines black consciousness and radical thoughts in a literary space and starts to get interesting.

After all, speculative fiction in Pacific literature is still an under-represented domain and our women writers needs serious representation.

I have been telling Dubo that although we have it in our traditional stories and we speak, recount and dramatise in the literary space fictional caricatures of folklores and legends, most indigenous writers in the country just never seriously engaged in it as literary discourse or a subjective area of interest to pursue, nurture and maintain. Like many other aspects of our socio-political cultures, we just never prioritised women in a development agenda.

I went on further to tell her that from the outset, there are just too many violent crimes and acts against women folk in society being reported in the media, that draws more public attention towards issues of gender inequalities in society.

Dubo is washing up after our breakfast as she listens to my long speech. She puts up with me now, since she went to college last year. Since she came back for holidays, my project, this work in progress, was a conversation, a staple form of intellectual dialogue for me. I enjoy picking her brain in how I was steering my novel.

It was one of those days but what made it more conducive was the wet cold rainy weather outside. The monsoonal season was at its peak and we were waiting for the brief interlude to go out to do our errands.

I continue on without a pause, "you know Dubo, more often at the forefront of gender as an agenda in development is the equity issues and gender-based violence. What about the human-interest angle of role models in society as a development challenge in the country from a literature perspective?"

"In other words, I guess what I am trying to say is that, what most critics and commentators overlook is that gender in 'development studies' is a complex subject to address in a multi ethnic society of diverse peoples, especially in creative fiction. Therefore, in the context of a writer, I want to move away from those traditional classical expectations of gender issues and to celebrate the indigenous perspectives of womanhood and feminine issues through a lived-in lens of Melanesian womanhood. How an indigene Bebeli woman looks at her life experience as a mother. By doing so I am interested in repositioning the lens at the different geopolitical perspectives of micro political structures at play in different settings of governance and social landscapes.

"Ok, mum I get it now, " Dubo intersects me as she turns on the electric jug. "You want the diaspora society experience for your main character, right?"

"Hmm, yes, from the lens of people from rural remote hamlets with a smaller, insular worldview. By adapting the community lens to major populous urban migrant settlement communities in the country, I want my characters to be portraits. After all, my intention is to show a contested SPACE of differing experiences and perspectives in a culturally changing landscape. A place of many memories whose residents' voices are vying to be heard, justified and validated accordingly; compared to the contemporary values of society and it's accepted norms or belief systems. That is why it is a novel with an intergenerational and relationship narrative."

"Sounds good Mama," she says as she gets up to make our coffee. Hubby has taken the other kids on those weekend grocery buying and errands. He stood at the kitchen door as we were conversing, giving hand signs to me about today's plans. Everyone knows why this is so important to me. The project is one of the outputs of the endangered languages revitalisation project for the Bebeli speaking tribe of West

New Britain Province, Papua New Guinea. Since then, this work in progress had taken off with such persevering determination. Working in such isolated support networks I have had to count on my family for support in field interviews and library research more often so they have all come to respect my space and time like today.

"I want this to be a prescriptive journey of reflectivity that mirrors different shades of colours that exists in our society", I continue on.

This is because I see misrepresentation as much as lack of translation. An inhibiting experience to our literary culture, our black literary fiction involving our black coloured people of a coloured person story; especially in Science Fiction. It is a prevalent experience where no matter where you come from some people just cannot go past the colour of your skin. African, Caribbean, Pacific Islander, Asian or a half caste - the judging of a person on their skin colour remains an aspect of human experience we go through in our global community.

"Now I am telling you Dubo, this here is not easy. No baby, it is not easy traveling this route. Since it recounts and relives those painful episodes of dark heritage involving Prejudice. These encounters weigh down the human heart that stoops too low to hear it. As much as every word has a scale, when we try to talk, we feel with our eyes the emotions in the words. Either spoken or read or left unmentioned in the test of time. That as much is the essence of memory and the will to survive. The magic that lies within these stories makes each experience a revelation that teaches us that to touch is to feel the savoury scents like an art piece gone with time."

"Huh!" I close my eyes and speak. "Just savouring each story is not easy my daughter," I tell her.

This is not an easy one in which an artist acting in the capacity of a writer uses. It derives much from the person (she or he) within their available intellectual capacity to tell a story that resonates throughout the passage of time. At the same time to retain indifference to the public reaction to it.

This is because the art of storytelling in itself is as much a form of public oratory of memory representing the ideals, voices and aspirations of a society. It transcends through generations and time as history. For if you ponder carefully, you will begin to understand it's very nature. It therefore presents an opportunity to either heal or destroy a world view of a narrative in a given frame and lens. The process towards this realisation weaves a paradox that can either make and remake leaders, or even belittle fools. It settles people back onto their 'places'.

"Do you think so?" Dubo asks with a frown, as she takes a sip from her cup.

"Yes, I do." I try to sound convincing. "This is because I want to believe that stories at a national and regional level are within their own different arrays of cultured tales, no more sung but told" I reply back.

"The irony in all this is that when we lose our indigene values and languages in our story telling opportunities we are on a path towards borrowing cultural representations out of our ignorance. How then can we sow for the future generations of our people our hopes, our dreams and aspirations as indigenous people in our Pacific blue ocean? This is a message that I want to relay in this narrative", I continue on.

"Come on now Dubo, isn't it obvious?" I add. The diaspora from within our homes starts to carve its own place within our voices and that further endorses the urgent need to tell our stories as indigenous people. "I know, Mama. I hear you. I feel you". She nods her head while I continue.

"Huh, girl listen to me. They are not just stories. These are our people's voices in the tide of time ebbing through the changing scene. Stories of hope, living and believing in good thoughts and deeds and just being the person we are. Often in telling these stories in our own voices we challenge formal history from a dominant cultural representation over other minority groups. For instance, in the context of black literary fiction, mostly the general audience perception is that it represents those within African countries and their diaspora communities throughout the world."

"Mama, it pains me you have never thought of becoming a literature tutor. This stuff they beg to be taught", she mumbles with a faraway look.

But I continue on with this reasoning. "Trying to put it all in the book. Let this novel be the teacher, the education system deprived me off. My story is no different to other middle-class housewives pushed out of the system for wantok cronyism in the bureaucratic Public Service system in this country. I am not going to be distracted from my literary dialogue either way".

It has been an undeniable fact that more often, other people of Black descent have had their stories either suppressed or ignored, and at times have been denied opportunities to tell them. The changing facets of our collective voices to maintain our self-worth and aspirations as a nation of a thousand tribes continues with despair. Thus they, and national institutions, fail to create spaces through which local citizens respond to change in their lives, assemble their lived-experience to face the future and at times to establish an indigene voice within the global community.

"In other words, our national creative literature when ignored by the national government suppresses the voices of ordinary citizens in our national social narratives. This in turn affects our issues of identity in indigeneity on how we define and identify our place in our society as a nation. Taking a 'generalisation' stance to identity through the highest office in government shows the depth of one's own indifference and ignorance. It starts with the micro political perspectives of how change imposes on the people's daily lives and that of their families."

"Oh Mama!, this sounds fantastic" Dubo's face lights up again in a wide grin. "So how are you going to create all this in the creative space? You know, the writer's question of what, why, where, who and when?"

"Huh, this is the part I was getting to and you interrupting me won't grasp the essence of my story telling," I complain.

The afternoon breeze is cool and calm like a gentle caress on my skin as the children and their father return home. Dubo pulls out vegetables for us to prepare dinner. I crack the coconut open watching the juice pour into the bowl. When it runs dry, I scrape it to shreds and later it will be used to cream the evening meal.

My Back ground In writing this novel

I am my own woman. That is who I am. I am tired of the label black, brown, coloured glaze, niggard woman. I am only human walking on this earth one time in my life time. That, that is who I am.

I don't know why I need to explain that over and over again. Trying to assert myself in this God forsaken land like some bad black odour in this world. This continual justification is not my vocation nor my calling but I am forever put there on the spot by my appearance. That presentation of being me. Just being me.

Now that I have said this statement, my being here making this grand entrance into our story: being women in our changing world from the small insular domestic family units to the wider world view of other cultures that look back at us with their own judgmental ways of acceptance and tolerance is really overwhelming for me. An indigenous Bebeli woman.

I was born a Korafe woman, born and raised, but I married a Bebeli man bore his children and I participate in his culture so I am as much a Bebeli woman.

I am a woman of substance. A daughter, sister, friend, lover, wife, colleague or even acquaintance. Even a stranger you pass on the street but whom you do not bother to know, minding your business in this busy world. I am a mother, someone's grandmother, the signature of which life starts to blossom and prosper on. In our Bebeli culture we are the doors towards the continuity of life's existence. A woman is the conduit of the life of society from one generation to another.

I don't see any reason why our stories should not be read. It is just *not being written* and told the way it is or should be. I cannot speak for everyone, just myself, and where I want to go from where I am as a person and valuable member of my society.

They say we woman have got stories but who hasn't? A woman just as much as anyone on this planet has got stories of life. I got to live for my children like my Mama did and her grandma did before her. That is the way of this world. That's why I am telling you my story - but my Mama and her Mama and my daughter they are all part of the thread that makes up our journey, the patchwork and embroidery of rich narratives. A bilum bag I had left back home.

Growing Up

My mother gave birth to me soon after the euphoria of independence was spreading around the country. I was the first of seven children and my childhood was one of privilege, more than most. My parents were among the many Papua New Guineans who became involved in the public service localisation program and growing up involved a lot travelling around Papua New Guinea.

My dad was one of the pioneers of the Papua New Guinea Defense Force Air Transport squadron and my early happy memories were the Christmas parties involving the toot toot train to the waiting DC3 aircraft that gave us a ride over the old Nadzab airport before we sat on Santa's lap and got our Christmas gifts.

Those were happy days for my brothers and I but it was overshadowed by the overwhelming sense of gloom from a reminder of how a dangerous fate could play on our father's military career through the events of the Vanuatu[4] campaign in the early nineteen eighties. Even several years now as an adult I can still feel the atmosphere of anxiety of getting dressed and going to welcome our dads for the homecoming.

There we were, all our mothers and us little children mostly toddlers huddled up in the huge troop carrier vehicle, our mothers' girlish voices giggling and fussing over our dresses with eager eyes. While we kids sat silently anticipating meeting the stranger whom mum endearingly reminded us was our dad. For most of us dad was the strange man who visited once in a while in that green army uniform. The man who hugged and kissed us hello and goodbye. Never staying, just forever working.

---

4   1980's Vanuatu independence was pending, and the French-leaning planters were aiding rebels to resist a smooth transition to independence. PNGDF troops went to Santo to replace the French and British who were leaving as fast as they could. The PNG force immediately went into action against the rebels resulting in a number of fierce firefights and casualties on both sides. Many prisoners were captured in the initial operation. These prisoners, both native people and French planters, were taken back to Vila in aircrafts for trial and imprisonment (they all asked to go to the French jail because wine was served with meals there). https://next-horizon.org/1980-memories-of-a-vanuatu-war/

Now there was excitement that he was returning from war. At the airport as the aircraft was circling the runway and making its last run, the atmosphere had reached its peak despite the military police giving us instruction on the program. Some mothers were already emotional and kids spotted their dads and waved, excitedly raising their voices. However, mum held the three of us together in front of her in dignified silence telling us that we had to respect dad. Keep our emotions under control until the military program was over. After all he was coming home.

When the military program was over, I remember dad hugging me as his tears rolled down and he spoke quietly "I'm home kids" it was then at that moment I recall mum crying. The silent unspoken joy of dad's homecoming.

We had many other happy memories travelling around military barracks in Papua New Guinea. However, it was Moem that has a special place for our family. It was at Boram hospital that my mother gave birth to my sister Rachel. Years later she would be stuck with the nick name "Sepik" in our family in memory of the place she was born. However, many times it caused a lot of curiosity from outsiders because of her Papuan features.

The place that we spent the later and major part of my childhood would be in Murray Barracks[5]. We moved into the barracks and were getting used to the city life when the Bougainville[6] civil conflict began. We became witnesses of the casualties of war, experienced the military curfews and the court martial media shut downs. The intense code of honour, silence and comradeship was also instilled in our hearts there.

---

5   National Capital District, Port Moresby, PNG. Ed

6   The Panguna mine is a large copper mine located in Bougainville. It is one of the largest copper reserves in Papua New Guinea and in the world, with an estimated one billion tonnes of ore copper and twelve million ounces of gold. BCL was majority owned by global mining group Rio Tinto, but operations ceased after the armed insurgency known as the "Bougainville Crisis". Significant and widespread environmental damage (which continues to this day,) and the limited financial compensation paid to landowners spilled over into a civil war that lasted a decade and claimed up to 15,000 lives. Ed.

Discipline and respect were the mast for attitudes our fathers taught us. Even when the Sandline[7] controversy gripped our fathers' loyalty we learnt the true word of nationhood. After all, we knew no other life in our childhood other than the homogeneous relationships we developed as "wantoks" in the barracks. Ours was the creation of a united Papua New Guinea through the children of the early service men in the Papua New Guinea Defense Force.

I was therefore part of that first generation of the diaspora population of the newly independent country of Papua New Guinea.

Mama's, Grandmother's And My Story

There was that certain glow of happiness in her eyes. Where the sunken flesh had been just a covering, it now had a certain smile that lit up her old face. The merest memory of it always brings tears to my eyes. For she had been through a lot in her life and achieved a lot, but this was the topping on the cake. In nineteen ninety-seven, my grandmother, Madeline Mota, graduated from her adult literacy course at Baga village near Tufi in Oro Province. It was a community program facilitated by the late Dr Cindy Farr, an American linguist involved in the Korafe-Yegha Bible Translation project of the Summer Institute of Linguistics.

My grandmother was in her late sixties with over 30 grandchildren from 11 of her own children but she wanted to achieve a lifelong ambition that had been denied to her many years before. This was the chance to read and write and the consequent opportunity to write a letter to her children in her own words.

---

7   The Sandline affair was a political scandal that became one of the defining moments in the history of PNG, and particularly the conflict in Bougainville. It brought down the government of Sir Julius Chan, and brought Papua New Guinea to the verge of a military revolt. Wiki

For some reason my grandmother never had a chance to go to school. The prospect was there when schools were built at Tufi in the early 1930s but there was mistrust among parents who would not let their daughters attend. My great-grandfather was one of those people and he would not approve her attendance. Instead, she grew up in the village spending time with her mother and the other women elders learning the traditional knowledge of our people through music, dance, craft and visual arts – as well as the secrets of the forest and natural environment, including their spirituality.

When she was in her late teens, my grandfather's relatives arranged for her marriage to my grandfather. My grandfather had married twice before and was older than her but she had no choice, it was the decision of the elders. From that marriage there were 11 children born but one was stillborn. Of the 10 who survived, my father was the eldest. My grandmother spoke a lot of the great changes that were happening in Tufi at that time. My grandfather had the chance to go to school and was employed in various capacities in the development program at the newly established Tufi government station.

When my dad was born, he had a humble upbringing at Baga village along with his siblings. He enrolled at Tufi Primary School and won a scholarship to attend Popondetta High School. While there, he enlisted in the Papua New Guinea Defense Force student cadet program and started a long career in the military. He was among the first Papua New Guineans in the Air Transport Squadron at Igam Barracks in Lae. Following in his footsteps, his younger brother, Anthony, enrolled at Popondetta High School and enlisted in the Royal Papua New Guinea Constabulary. He began a lifelong career in the police force.

My father and Anthony left home as two young men who my grandmother willingly released to serve their country. During those years of separation, communication became a personal struggle where letters were the only means of staying in contact. However, because she could not read or write, my grandmother relied on others to write and read her letters. Sometimes there was nobody willing to do this. At other times people misinterpreted what she wanted to say and sometimes people told lies in the letters. She also relied on grandfather but as he grew older his eyesight began to fail. So, she took up the challenge to learn to read and write for both of them.

When the Korafe-Yegha bible project started in Baga village in the 1960s, my grandfather became very much involved in the literacy programs, attending the writers' workshops and often illustrating some of the books that were published. During those times, grandmother would silently wish she could one day participate in the training. Through Dr Cindy Farr's persistence and the encouragement of the Korafe women, my grandmother was able to learn to read and write. It took a lot of convincing for the men in the village to let the women attend the classes. After all, our Korafe society is very patrilineal.

The classes were held in the morning and at first the men were a bit apprehensive. Many turned up on the first day and, when the morning tea break bell rang, grandfather jokingly remarked that there were a lot of excited men outside the classroom curious to see how their wives' classes were progressing. Classes ended at midday so the women could do their chores. Grandfather recalled it was a very challenging time where the roles of men and women were tested. By the end of the first week, several women pulled out, but for those who continued until the completion, the program was a triumphant occasion for them and their husbands and families.

Soon after completing the program my grandparents visited us in Port Moresby and it was the highlight of their news. I was so proud of her achievement because I was her eldest granddaughter and doing my first year at the University of Papua New Guinea.

She had encouraged my father to allow his daughters to reach their highest potential in education and she was a shining example of the motto "education is a lifelong journey".

It was there and then that I began to value adult literacy programs. Many years later I am still developing resource materials and learning aids for adult literacy training in the remoter areas of Papua New Guinea. Some of the remote groups I have visited to conduct literacy training are Moreguina Saint Jude's and Saint Simon's Anglican Mothers Union at Cape Rodney in Central Province, Zenag village in the Mumeng District of Morobe Province and Amgoreng and Gimi villages, both in West New Britain Province.

My grandmother's achievement influenced not just me but many others in the family, including my mother. My mother had retired from a very successful and long career in property management to complete her college degree. She jokingly remarked that she wanted her grandchildren to know that she had completed a college degree. I remember very well because it was when I was in labour with my first child. I asked her once what it was like to be in a class with young people as old as her own children and she replied that it is the person and their dreams that matter.

Soon after graduating with a Business Administration degree, my mother, along with my dad, were engaged by the Anglican Church to conduct adult literacy training programs in the remote villages of the Jimi Valley and Koinanambe in the highlands. Today they are very much involved in the Summer Institute of Linguistics Korafe-Yegha Bible translation project started by Dr Cindy Farr and her husband Jim Farr so many years ago. Dr Farr passed away in 2008 and my grandmother passed away soon after. However, their legacy for our Korafe-Yegah women and indeed for PNG continues.

Now I coordinate a special community inclusive learning education program at Callan Services West New Britain Province. It's a volunteer program imparting life skill and knowledge to people living with disabilities, unemployed youth and women who want to learn new skills to earn income for their families. It is a unique program we are trialing to develop a social intervention strategy to address adult literacy issues in the province. There are many challenges in this work but it is still an interesting job. One I dedicate to my grandmother, Madeline Kitako.

My Story

There was nothing she could do now but pack. They would take their two back packs and the blue weather-beaten suitcase. The bare minimum of their lives that they could carry with them. Everything would now be in the past tense. Now all that mattered was going forward together. To a new beginning. A new destination from that day onwards.

Just the thought of it made her weak with anxiety yet there was no other day. It was either now or never she had to remind herself every few minutes as the time moved towards the boarding call. Overhead the public announcement system continued to give directions to the travelers as hordes of passengers moved into the departure lounge waiting for their boarding calls.

Together they sat, mother and daughter, side by side looking out the glass window to the sun rise. It's radiance from the mountain tops of the Motuan landscape hovering at a distance towards Jackson international Airport, was a soothing caress for them. The mother's stiff slender frame relaxed towards the little girl as she leant on her in return.

They looked alike with the pale Polynesian complexion and dream like huge eyes. Their big fuzzy hair braided in identical twin braids were neatly clasped into a bun with a hair band.

The cold morning had now been replaced by the scorching rays of the new day. She could feel that soggy sensation of body heat and grit from the city dust, it's cracked freckles on her body. Her lips were dry and coarse as flakes clung to her lips. But it was the thought of hunger that worried her the most.

The road was long and it was hot so she prayed her daughter, Caitlin would not cry. From pre morning until day break they sat looking at the terminal screen waiting for the boarding call. They had not had breakfast. They only had those loose coins she had for their fare to get them to their final destination.

She was aware that Caitlin was a late sleeper and had woken early to take this flight so she had become more vigilant over her. She was praying that their flight would arrive at their destination trouble free. She tried not to fuss over her, engaging her in conversations to get her mind off food. Her braids swinging on her head whilst she made little stands, skips and jumps watching the crowd ebb and flow around her.

The departure lounge was crowded with a diversified lot of travellers taking the early morning flights. It was always ebbing back and forth as departure calls were made and boarding passengers exited the boarding gates. A moving mass of people in transit. All around and everywhere they were surrounded by little dramas unfolding and flowing in the tide of time. It was like a big expanse of overwhelming void and presence pressing onto them, just watching them unfold; all at the same time.

All around there were stern looking well-dressed people in business suits fiddling with their phones and making long calls in between. Across from them there were those crowds of tearful and solemn people saying their farewells. They looked like they were either friends or family members taking leave from each other. Near them there were some people with happy faces who had those genuine grins plastered across their faces with that air of surging hope, adventure and blustering eagerness and impression of one looking forward to the journey and counting every second till the departure call. The other lot were those grim uncertain unsmiling lot that looked like weary travellers tired and bored by their surroundings. They were just waiting, sitting quietly and looking at the terminal screen for the boarding call announcement.

Everyone was oblivious to what others were feeling, experiencing and they were also trying to cope with their own anxiety issues in completing their journey. Some people coming and going to the kiosk at the end of the lounge where hot and cold beverages were on sale with light snacks and sandwiches.

People moved to the lavatories at the back too. Whilst a continuing stream of new travelers entered the lounge looking around to take a seat. It was always a very busy place of people passing each other, sitting across from each other and finally walking up to the boarding gate to take their flight.

It was a routine she had grown up in as a daughter of someone who worked all his life in the airline industry. She had also traveled frequently in business trips as a professional artist but this was different kind of travel. A trip that she was taking with her daughter and eldest child.

To that new place. A new beginning. If ever there was a time she could think as the most impressionable in her life, this was it. The uncertainty of the unknown and to take the risk to change the narrative of their lives from a single parent home to a real family. She had been praying long and hard to have that quiet assurance that God was watching over them.

When they arrived, they took a seat in the front rows of the lounge area so Caitlin could watch the planes take off and land to at least take her mind off food. She had packed her water bottle and some biscuits for this trip but Caitlin had since consumed it all.

Now all she wanted to do was sleep shuffling her drowsy self across the benches trying to find a good spot to take a nap. They had arrived at the airport just before day break where darkness still enveloped the place and the terminal was well lit inside with a much smaller crowd. They were early and ready to take this trip checking in at the counter before entering the boarding lounge. Together they watched the time pass and the sun appear over the Koari hill sides overlooking the airport runways. They had been waiting at the airport for two hours now.

In her mind she kept trying to contain the rationality of her decision repeating to herself, " I started this." Still trying to see, though she cannot see but only hear verses singing in her head like triple jumping into creativity. She lost her colours in the beat, so back to the drawing board waiting for the journey ahead.

The morning light had shone through the glass window making them move again but it was getting near to departure time now. She kept her hand tightly on Caitlin as the crowd rose and dwindled with each boarding call.

Caitlin was getting restless, getting up and walking around the small space, standing still and looking back at the crowd. She was a picture of an innocent child clad in her blue denim jeans and pink tee shirt her hair braided in two rows and that now was clasped with two matching pink hair bands, unaware of the anxiety and emotions running through her mother's heart. She had made a decision to live and to move on not just for herself but also for her daughter. Finally, the announcement to board their flight was made. So she carried both their bags and stood in the line to get their boarding pass.

This was it. They were finally moving on. Starting all over again leaving behind the past. A new beginning, new life. Far away from here. They were going home to Hans and starting a family. Leaving Port Moresby for Kimbe.

Here where the public oratory heals or destroys and makes leaders and belittles fools, our cultural tales are no longer sung because the people now borrow then sow their experiences into homogeneous packages. Is it not correct, the critics complain, that Melanesians have lost touch with their blood lines and culture? A diaspora bubble rising and growing like a brew, bubbling and oozing as if just waiting and reeking in its wake. About to and ready to, at its pending optimum peak; burst.

So now we young mothers are grasping for the seams of truth, like dark shades, hovering in the back drop. But then again, is it not Values that have changed with time, and not the colour of blood? So, what is heritage defined when you let outsiders preach down on you. Is it not a lesson to know the roots from which you descend where dark shades remain.

Now as a mother tending to my child, I contemplate our future. Yes, I remember the future and like others the promise of new beginnings. Looking back now I acknowledge that the life I have had is like a collage with pieces of pleasures, triumphs and loss as much as the pain and laughter. With stitches from hard knocks through tears and wonder. How time flies by unaltered on its path. As all this has woven a beautiful patchwork that shines here and there with a verse to share together.

And every day in its receding years the future was becoming like the Adder it was. Not that I want to preach about my eyes but still. Someone was enjoining two or three fragmented lives into one family every night at the prayer meetings without knowing it. God knows how much she wanted to please him in her prayers but it was a subtle grace working in this line of living.

Miracles happen every day at every turn. You start to develop this complacent attitude to wrongs and think it's a godly right to receive blessings every other way. The biggest poison of one's faith is that unwavering faith of a Christian soldier. Have we seen it all? We have, but we just never grow up to notice it's Character traits. That was how it was like then, taking that leap and taking Caitlin to a new life all those many years ago.

I want so much of this to work it was like stitching a promise of hope within our marriage union. That was how she had justified her decision. The sacrament of Holy Matrimony where together we promise to travel when she had committed to him. A life time of shared memories that was what it promised then and still is. This is how she describes her decision. A journey of life through the deep vale where dim light casts shadows on our path so we will stand side by side. Sifting through the hurt and tears in between the pandemonium.

This is someone with whom I want to be able to trust in order to find my voice because he stands close to my heart. It is as if I am led to him across the vast oceans. Nothing seems to be able to stand in my path, even when dusk descends to dim the path I cannot imagine otherwise. What then would life be without you, my family. For you are the core of my happiness and life.

The Port Moresby they had left was a different place back then. A growing metropolitan town with its own distinct character. The home of a thousand tribes of people who live and work there, it was growing a culture of a modern Papua New Guinea diaspora population, uprooted and separated from their own ethnic groups and ancestral homes.

The more educated the younger generation, the more dissident voices sprouting among the mass citizens. The Civil rights movement was starting to gather momentum as information technology and social media opened doors to opportunities, whilst bringing the global community to its door step.

Change had been a great leap with considerable sacrifices by all our national leaders for a sovereign state. It was a time our country was stepping out into the global trade market as one of the promising young nations in the Pacific region.

Caitlan and I were leaving all these advances in living standards behind for a much quieter environment. The village life of family bonding and re- engagement. Local heritage of traditional bonding and knowledge of the indigenous life of our people. I wanted to settle down and I had made a decision to move on.

My daughter's story

Now they were here again where it all began. The same airport but different design and architecture. All upgraded and modernised to meet the needs of the new generation of travelers. Though the physical spaces have changed they were doing the same function absorbing the same emotions of its clients passing through its gated enclosure. Now the biggest differences were the security and better ablution facilities. The waiting lounge and departure terminals were now better fitted than the time they had first arrived.

She was ready with her suitcase and backpack. This time they were separating. This time it was her and Hans doing the tearful farewell to Caitlin. Her daughter was no longer the little girl that accompanied her around all her life today was the day they would make that break. She was now a young adult going off to a new beginning. Making a new direction, a new start in her own life. Now this is where the break was starting. She was going off to take up studies at the university in another province.

It was the first time she was going to take a long trip on her own. Leaving behind all that she was used to and the comfort her family life. It was going to be a beginning, new life and a new journey to her new future as an adult. All around them there were other students with their families. All of them going through their own emotional farewells. They had arrived early but a long queue was already there at the check in counter. Security was strictly enforced but allowed parents and guardians in to assist the new traveling students.

The weather was cold and chilly but it was a midday flight. Monsoonal rains were threatened, and now back clouds hovered high above as darkness descend in gentle layered hues like dooming gloom blooming looming bringing sounds of rustling leaves. Rushing past in a breeze never stopping as the scene unfolds everywhere. Below the forest floors await. Flashing splinters race across the open sky as droplets fall. Curtains rise and fall in crescendos. Living beauty of nature calls beyond, beckoning rise with its splendour, and appears with clapping feats of roaring pride spreading their spell of monsoonal showers sobbing in deep grieving.

In this heart rending few minutes we sat there with nothing else to do but just wait.

An announcement was made that the flight was going to off-load some passengers so it triggered a lot of scrambling, shoving and arguments for those who had not received boarding passes.

Caitlin had received a partial government scholarship to study Agriculture Sciences at the University in Lae so her trip was funded in this package. She was among the fortunate few given a boarding pass. They were given priority over others due to their registration dates scheduled for the university academic year calendar.

As the hours turned into minutes, they let her go into the departure lounge. Waiting outside on the car park they saw her walk up to the aeroplane. There were other parents as well, saying their farewells. Hans turned to her and they both watched as the plane sped down the runway before lifting into the sky.

She was on her way now. To a new beginning. A new start in her life. Forging her place in the academic life of the university.

"*Goodbye Caitlin,*" they whispered softly as they shed their tears while looking over the horizon as the plane flew up into the sky.

Caitlin's mother whispered softly in her mother tongue a mother's prayer. The same prayer her mother whispered to her when she went off to school almost two decades ago and her mother before her. Now she understood what it was like when a mother said her farewells to her child. The endearing moment of departure and moving onwards in life.

*"Nanda gargara, dubo jamaghe yasi", *she repeated silently as Hans held her hands to comfort her. (My daughter, go in peace)*[8].

Next to her, other parents also shed their tears; it was life changing for all of them. Letting them go out into the world to carve their own path and destiny.

Like a spectrum before them the aeroplane took off from the runway lifting into the sky, its engines roaring out loudly as it throttled and rumbled into the dark dim skies. Within minutes it became a tiny dot and disappeared beyond the horizon and from their gaze. Turning to look at each other they walked to the bus stop to make the journey home.

The wet weather was as damp as the emotions ebbing from within. A light drizzle of rain drops fell on them as they walked to the bus stop and the afternoon crowd was at its peak. School children lined the roadside trying to get a ride home. Their chatter and giggles rang out in the crowded bus they got on. On the way they had to steer around the big pothole puddles on the road, as the rain drops got more violent and insistent. It was getting dark and cold as they offered silent prayers for Caitlin to get to her destination safely.

Home was a distance across those silver linings that met the ocean, blue lines over the sea a sinking longing that haunts the viewer looking out especially when you are far from home. Many an evening walk by the beach, it calls out to bystanders and when you look it seems to sing in that silent tune of emotions. Playing magic in your wake bringing to the brim a pressing sense for the familiar. A longing for dear ones far away in homes across the ocean.

As the final lights fade away to the looming dusk with that majestic grace of the final bow, splashing waves bid farewell in the surging

8 *Korafe language, Oro province, Papua New Guinea*

tides as another day ends. In that passage of the fading light where the moon starts to make her grand entrance, a seagull flies above the sea in a hasty retreat. Swirling and calling out to the day's keepers that the end of another day is now accomplished. It has ended in dark murmurs of the nocturnal gaze whose deep sighs breathe in unison of grace that was ever so close and morose, the tail of the day.

It is the wettest month of the year now. The cold draughts at night sting our bones and rattle our teeth as we cling onto the threadbare bedsheets. During daylight it is muddy and soggy outside. Debris is swept by the tide of over flowing drains onto roadsides and foot paths while pedestrians run past them in hurried strides. There's something about the way people cope with the weather in order to meet their deadlines or complete tasks.

It is just the way we had come to send off our child Caitlin. Despite whatever circumstances we were facing we had to let her go and face the world. She had to forge her way into and through the storm surrounding our lives. Little did we expect that in this turn of events we would also be starting our own journey as her parents within our own storm in our own social landscapes. The new beginning of something promising in the near future by our child's expectations.

It was not the way of our people, the indigene way of doing things. This sending off a girl child travelling on her own to pursue a life so different from our own. Times have surely changed very much.

What our tears shed is the loss of youth, the sacrifice of personhood for a higher pursuit. The tear drops flow in time with memories.

We built a family home over the years with hope, aspirations and the promise to a future together. Children were born, alliances were made as they grew old together and Caitlin went on to university overseas.

From that time when we had arrived until Caitlin's departure just now, our little village had undergone huge changes. We lived in   the centre of an ebbing tide of large-scale commercial Agriculture activities. Economic migrants flooded our village, that surrounded the fringes of the Provincial town. With this rising migration tide there were emerging voices of contested spaces. In the midst of this our people were losing their awareness of "place" and the interconnectedness they used to have. Blood continued to spill from our youth as the traditional haus boi system started to lose its place among our youths. The worst of it all was the impression of having the need to identify their own mother tongue from pidginisation.

The changing landscapes have become the essence of the grassroots emancipation in a contested environment between migrant settlers and the indigenous people. The stinging reality for the need to re-imagine a security zone to determine the sprawling and the rising cost of living. Wherein the government creates an illusion of a martial rule of curfew restrictions on the province. It was no longer the place we had envisioned it to be. A quiet place to raise a family. We are seriously considering moving further inland to avoid the crowd.

My Journey As An Artist/ Story teller

I remember how restless and impatient I had been. That sheer weight of not knowing how it would turn out was pressing down on my mood heavily. The jostling bumpy ride added to my growing litany of irritations building up inside me but the clean open breeze was a soothing balm on my nostrils. It was all so surreal, while the breeze was calming me with its refreshing coolness. It was my first commissioned art job after leaving school and I was already panicking. I was on duty travel and it meant a lot at that time, being an artist.

Somehow in being calm sitting there staring into the distance as the ebbing currents dissipated into the pit of my stomach I had not realised how my neatly brushed hair was unceremoniously loosened, blown and ruffled in the wind. I had been drawn towards the passing scenes of emerald carpet clad hill where at some intervals there were notches etched from within the nooks and crannies fast flowing rivers cascaded down in graceful strides. Never rushing or missing a beat just gently passing over the various paths it meandered on.

I sometimes recall how it had been a long and winding road we traveled that morning. It seemed to me that day was stretching on and on, a never-ending stretch disappearing into the horizon beyond. Nestled within it was the breath-taking scenery of the Morobean hinterland. The Markham highway and Mumeng valley in all its magnificence were a sight to behold.

After a long ride we arrived at our destination in mid-morning. There was a welcome procession before we conducted our community survey. That proceeded onto a farewell meal and we were back on the journey to Lae city.

Forever imprinted in my memory from that day back in the late nineteen nineties it did not seem like a big fuss at that time but now looking back, it was a start of life long career of community development through art engagement roles I had undertaken over the following years.

Almost three decades on I have traveled across continents, the Pacific Ocean and lived in local hamlets and villages in some remote rural areas of the country developing training, advocacy and literacy resources for local communities. Reflecting back to that first experience there were not many indigenous women artists at that time. Certainly not many engaged in community development programs in their capacity as a professional visual artist so it was an eye-opening experience. Not just for me but for many people I encountered through my professional journey.

Now in Ruango village.

The skies have cleared and the morning dew glistens under the bright morning rays. The soggy wetness is starting to rescind into the lofty mountain ranges as we hang the wet mouldy laundry out to dry. The kitchen is filled with smoke from the breakfast fires with the brewing tea pots and the aluminium pots. Dented blackened and reshaped from original forms to fit into the household character of its users. The hard biscuits and hot tea breakfast was quickly consumed as we hurried off to our field site.

The sea tide was coming in and we had to wade through the Rowo River on the way. Me carrying the recording equipment on my head so it didn't get wet. A lot of debris was banked on the beach shores. Too early, too soon, to clean up in this wet weather. We walk over it on our way to crossing Tawaki River again. The same thing happens when I hold up the bag carrying my equipment and cross the river. I look with sadness over our neglected block in front.

Overgrown shrubs and weeds have drowned it with unruly abandonment. For a passing moment an ache gnawed deep within me: when am I going to attend to this domestic chore?

We walk past it somehow, eventually getting to Kedo Wakapi our Agriculture block. Behind the copra shed is my work space. There in the open space of the coconut plantation estate is the comfort of nature all around. Clean fresh air and the calm look of butterflies, insects and birds chirping in the trees.

My qualifications to write my own personal journey has been the life I have lived.

Part 1

Na Vironu Sedo, dubo kotise anumbirena.

(I recall with fondness the memories as I ponder with a reflective gaze).

Prologue: The Watcher (from Mila's email)

The day the wind spirit arrived in our lives in our village was the day you went away for your university studies. That was what Mama said. She never stops talking about it.

Caitlin, it is just me and Dido. She tells this story as if there's something hidden inside the story itself. Dido gets tired of listening to it and gives her the silent treatment. Walking off on some errands and disappearing soon after.

No, she doesn't tell Papa. She says she doesn't want to bore him with the details of misery when he is so tired after making his many rounds of copra production. These are spiritual matters that men cannot handle, she argues, so Papa is spared these mumbling grumbling sessions at home.

It is about the ongoing phenomena of spiritual matters involving our domestic space, evident from an invasion by rodents. Mama is convinced that it is some kind of a spiritual warfare on our doorsteps. These, combined with other matters, mean that she is convinced of a higher paranormal activity in our home environment. We are all perplexed by her sudden interest in the matter. She does have some convincing points though, with all these strange incidents happening in the house. Papa does not seem affected by all these though, and does not even want to know.

Mama says "Since you went away, we began to realise certain actions of others towards us in the village. How they treated us when we were around them. Then we became conscious of ourselves when we were in their presence. Somehow our narratives changed the day you left home. We felt the pinch of our dire circumstances too, trying to make ends meet so you can achieve your dreams and goals. Every day we lived a hand to mouth existence. We scraped through the days so food could be put on the table. We all begged to survive. It was as if the scent of poverty stretched its long talons on our wealth trying to drown us into debt. How did we come to this stage is a question that has been haunting us ever since. Despite all the prayers and soul-searching pleas, we were left to drown in the surging tide that was spiraling before us. In this state of self-consciousness, we were more alert of our own circumstances compared to that of those around us."

It was as if a supernatural presence had been unleashed over our lives. Our Christian analogy would be interpreted as saying that evil sat on our roof eating up goodness and the prosperity of our family. From the pit her evil belly she gnawed at our efforts. She taunted us mercilessly despite our pleas and through no fault of us she tugged and pulled in all directions to destroy us. We cried and begged Saint Michael the archangel and pleaded with God the Father and the Holy Trinity to take this plague that fell upon us. We noticed the sizes of the rats that came at night to our house and ate the new clothes we bought. We noticed the huge toads that squatted as sentinels at our stairs. We saw Tamana Gelu watching our every movement like an insane man. The stalking psychopath in our neighbourhood."

"This was the watcher looking down on us and trying to use its psychological evil eyes to eat out the goodness in our home. We sent back a thousand-fold all the snakes, scorpions and evil intent of his heart back to his home and family. Through the blood of Jesus Christ our Lord and Saviour we pledged cleansing and healing grace in our family over our finances and prosperity."

"It was uncanny really, how our finances became less and the need to make ends meet became a struggle. We seemed to realise how our situation became more dire and our circumstances more desperate with each passing day. We were more alert and aware of this than ever before. It was as if the evil sat perched on our roof top redirecting our wealth and fortune furiously as we embarked on trying to change our family narrative and that of our people. To some extent within the perspective of our Christian belief we acknowledged our new circumstances as going through a spiritual battle field in the spiritual realm as we waded through the situation that was rewriting our family history. It was a situation that made our senses alert to local fashion and materialistic consumption trends and choices."

"We also noticed how people started to flaunt their lifestyle before us. How they looked down at us knowing that we were struggling. As a family we all went into our own pits of humility trying get out of this cycle of financial shortage trying to drown us."

"We became more convinced than ever that it was not normal. In fact, it was evil at its worst state. Here we were so busy trying to put food on the table as the grass grew on the lawn and the weeds wind spent and dusty became scraggly foot paths on our door step. The clothes on our backs became rags. Doors began to shut to us. It was like a death spell was unleashed on us. It devoured every goodness from within our family."

"As I write, the sweeping willows howl relentlessly outside my windows."

"It's been raining unceasingly these past few days as if it's any explanation of their keening. They are being tossed and getting rattled by the frenzy of the storm. Getting mixed up into the melee of the wind and rain dancing up to the flashing streaks of the lightning. It is as if the Gods are engaged in a deep row or sorts. The chaotic chatter and rush of pandemonium from the weather. It is something to behold, living through it. This blistering raging fireworks of nature continuing nonstop. Bickering continuously like women arguing over betel and mustard as the cold air tosses and turns in an avalanche of bursts and splattering like a maiden tossing her hair in the wind. It is as if there is no end in sight of this natural calamity."

"On our island the old people remind us that everyone came with the same song but each had their own tune and melody. Like the morning bird that praised the new day. Plants bloom in their greatness but it is us humans that lost the ways of praising the richness of life to live in it."

"It has been raining for several days now non stop. Just that endless heavy thrashing and crashing water from the sky. Those intermittent pauses in between the growl, rumble and roar in quick succession of bursts, streaks and flashing light. Sudden and illuminating in the dark. An invisible battle fought on our turf without us seeing, as silhouettes stretched out in the shadows trying to claw away our skin with draughts of chilling air. The weather resonates with our emotional issues here. It is like being in a dark spectre of the supernatural powers beyond our control. We were under spiritual attack in a battle field we were unprepared and ill equipped to handle. A battle of wills raged within us on our paths. We were like puppets on a stage being drawn into a play in whose script we could not rehearse but only improvise along the away."

"These shocking fresh insights into our lives are like a new awakening. Realisations that people we respected as friends wear masks before us and reveal their true voices when our circumstances change. In the midst of our troubles their rear heads appeared when their expectations are not met. Issues you faced have become public broadcasts in the village. In recent weeks this has brought out a lot of people 's hidden feelings towards you and us as a family."

"Here on the island not many people go to university. This is the backwater of civilization. Even though our people are the traditional custodians, our government has kept us as invisible citizens on Official Records. Our island was the headquarters of German New Guinea and the colonies of the German Imperial Government in the Pacific Islands."

"In a way, you going away has given rise to a mixture of envy, shame and pride like a bitter taste on our historical narratives."

"A minority indigenous person having a university education in our culture is like a powerful post for his or her people; is it not a good target or candidate for sorcery? The ancient art of evil soothsayer, magicians and witch doctors are part of that mix of society's undesirables in our midst. They form a special class of people where fortunes build or fall. One that no sane person wants to provoke to become the enemy."

"Now", Mama was convinced, "it has jinxed its way into our family assets and natural wealth like a bad luck charm".

Chapter 1

Avia Agira

The laulau* trees rustled gently against the afternoon breeze as willy wagtails chirped on their branches under the blue sky with the open sea a crimson shade. It glistened as men and women went about their chores leaving behind in the village the old, the frail, the sick and children. As usual in the mid-morning light the sound of children's voices and peals of laughter resonated all around whilst the older children attended to their daily chores. In her little hut, old Makuri hummed a soft tune in her head with a faraway look on her face.

The lahara* wind had started to dance again last night. Tossing and tearing things in its path. It was a time when the river bed was cracking. Opening its jaws in the remorseless heat. The merciless dry weather had been too hard and longer than usual. The old people in the village called it baimara*, the season of deep hunger. There were many such incidents in living memories but none worse than that of the time when the sun refused to shine. The food crops wilted and the air was filled with rotting corpses as life left them. It was a reign of misery with such hollowed restlessness. An unsettled evil drinking goodness from all around weighing hard on the human spirit. Dull unrelenting ache.

Gone were the people's labour of harvesting, as barren fields lay desolate and deserted. There were no more tears, no cries, but the desolate emptiness of despair. It was a defeated scene and vile deeds leered in the backdrop. It all came back to the survival of the fittest. In this instance, the resilience of the human spirit to face adversity. In that dark calamity the old people of the old world survived to tell of it. Their peoples' greatest survival story in the time of deep hunger.

This was one of her people's good time stories. Stories that connect the *knowing* to the people. About time past and hope sought, built and pursued by our people. But it was a story built upon stories and buried in people hearts until woken for a purpose.

Old Makuri shook her head as if to free her head of some weight pressed down on her, bringing her thoughts to the present sound of children playing nearby. The faint rustling of swaying coconut palms outside her hut made her look at them more intently. They seemed to stand aloof like loyal soldiers on parade. Behind them, in the backdrop, the scruffy cocoa trees looked like ill-mannered neighbours loudly stating their dissatisfaction of life with their dust blown leaves on straggly branches. Looking further into the distance, the hillside of Mount Hobohobo peered down on the village.

In recent days, the once abundant forest with its myriad beautiful treasures had become a shadow of its former self. It's scrawny bones protruding to the heavens like sculptures of beggars pleading for crumbs.

To old Makuri it was a sign of a bad omen. Of some dark visitation about to befall the earth. She was not the only one with this premonition. Through the village and miles away the old people started remembering the dark days of hunger and its searing weight of memory. Nature was speaking its own rude knowing. The coming doom.

Here in Tangana Pogi, old Makuri was one of the village elders that the village people sought to read the signs in nature as the days stretched into a prolonged dryness. The men in the village discussed great survival schemes for the looming drought as women made plans for food rationing. The art in music, dance and craft which brought back nostalgic memories of the good times was now replaced by deep tones of longing and weariness. The surging sinking tone of a desolate wanderer seeking answers to a present demise prevailed. Yet this was her parents' story from her ancestral lands way out over the distant seas and horizon

The story of the Korafe people of Tufi, Oro province. They don't belong here. A place surrounded by the sea in the middle of the Pacific Ocean. But then again, it was hard now attaching lessons to a landscape as it cascades through your mind with all the other memories. There and then she remembered how it was. The long piercing pain in her heart that tries to swallow her in the dream. The emptiness of longing. Remembering home and all that it represented to her. A place where love was boundless and secure.

A hamlet where the old women in the family cooked *"papara"*, the baked sago scones or *"simbari"* sago porridge laden in thick coconut cream and sang the *baimara** songs. The deep enchanting lyrics whose melodies rang into the starry night with their magical chords playing on people's hearts. Sometimes and more often, too stirring emotions, bringing tears and disquieting feelings of helplessness. At times it made you wonder out aloud, "Surely the wind will change, won't it?" or is it just a matter of time before the wet season will come again? Ha, thus was the unspoken words because it was the place of the old people to speak.

Old Makuri remembers it all though. These days in her old age it all comes back like a pack of files. A photographic film with the smell and emotions stirring deep within. It is all like a long journey away from where she sits and lives now. Another part of the country, and in another time. Years and years ago.

To her she would always remain the outsider. A woman who left her people for the man she married. Here she remained bearing his children and serving his people. But she knew to never forgot who she was and the culture she had left behind. Over the years she had started to see the similarities and the likenesses that exist. How deep these roots grew into you and made sense of life. Like now as she sat listening to the women elders singing in the moon light the traditional dance Reiki of the Bakovi tribe.

Today they are doing a message on the time of drought, when a grave famine swept across the plains of New Britain island through the lens of a traditional dance called, *reki**.

> Oh, my dearest *pupu**, here I sit and ponder the passing days and impressions in these words as in reminisce, *Vironu**. A statement of a lost time in my own foreign tongue of Korafe language where the mighty talented Kotofu women made elegies of time pasts. Ha!, and they were great poets when they had their way. Huh, how they recited the phrase, *Na Vironu sedo, dubo kotise Irena.* (I spoke remembering aloud, the depth of my memory of the life I had lived.)

Salim tingting tasol taim karai blo solwara buruk lon nambis na em silip sore. Pisin iplai antap lo em na lukluk strong lon em. Tasol tingting blo mi go long wei tru. Aburusim mak blo ai blo mi taim mi salim tingting lon Peles. Mama na papa, brata Susa peles long wei Turu na mi marit long wei tumas. Na taim mi harim nek na lap blo ol pikinini bel bilong mi kirap gen. Laip swit moa tu. Mi kamap olsem pisin blo solwara Mekim mauswara na solwara buruk lon iau blo mi. Aiyo solwara yu silip sore tumas.

(*To reminisce with the echoes of waves crashing onto the sea shores here I sit on the beach where the sea birds fly high above and look down on us. The calm and gentle sound of crashing, rushing water hitting the sand banks creates a gentle note of longing. A dull ache buried deep within me soars and sears my peace of mind making me homesick. How I miss the presence of my father, mother and siblings. The distance that stands between us is the marital status of my life. In the happy moments of family life my memories of home become a distant past. The bitter joys of living. Now if only I were a seabird, I would fly high up aboveI sing of praises that resonate like waves echo. Oh how you lie in gentle serenity*).

What would our village be like ten years from now?

This is a sad question to ponder. Here the land stands desecrated into the abyss of madness. The ruthlessness of land grabbing wrangling and validation of these acts of hegemonic acts are as naked as the bare rays of the sun. Bright and raw in the public glare to develop and colonise groups of indigenous people on their own ancestral lands. These intrusions and invasions in the name of nationhood move to erase our cultural identity and also relationships with our land. The emancipation of our people remains a silent resistance through the collective imagination of the people.

They held onto their customs and traditional practices to retain their awareness of places and their significance of their connections to the land and sea. For many generations this had been an effective socio-cultural movement of resistance to the invasion of their traditional spaces.

Avia Agira tells us that development of our land has been on the basis of land grabbing and monetisation of land. Thus, the continuous and gradual displacement and disinheritance of many of our peoples' rights to access our ancestral homeland. As a consequence, successive government bureaucrats have disregarded the indigenous Bebeli people and their socio cultural and economic rights and benefits derived within the development plans of the town. To an extent they have become mere spectators of the development taking place on their customary land. This has escalated land disputes and in turn affected identity issues for inheritances. This further disrupts the provision of goods and services in the town when clans dispute. Our tribe is an indigenous marginalised community in the Province without any official recognition in the Provincial government.

We continue to face a new wave of legal battles every year. Identity theft issues regarding our people representation abound. It is brewing because lawyers and government officials are buying our traditional and customary land and forming a syndicate that moves to land grab our land by means of creating laws that give greater authority to acts of land grabbing. Meanwhile, pop-up clans have emerged becoming social miscreants in our society. To such an extent they have built up a growing momentum to drum up compensation claims for our customary lands to the government. Over our land.

In our village this is becoming a constant socio-political challenge of powerlessness where new court charges are continuing to be issued to Pupu No'oh. These are instigated with violent confrontation from Rambo and his elder brother and their bands of little gangs in the village settlements. The conspiracy by a major agricultural company to impose the use of user rights policy documents on unsuspecting illiterate villagers to grab and acquire customary land has now backfired on them when more settlement farmers are now planting rival cash crops to their commercial crop.

On the national scale, the special economic zone areas by the current incumbent government are an issue we tread with in trepidation. Considering that it is cooperatives other than land owners who are recognised in these business ventures that require acquisition of land and maritime spaces from local villagers.

However, the sad irony in all this wrangling is that here in Kimbe we have a series of Plantocratic regimes, with an historical legacy of exploitation of indigenous peoples' rights. Thus, the colonial land grabbing and monetisation of land and its natural environment resources. So much so that it is an undeniable fact that we live in an environment that does not respect and value a person's life. This is a place where money talks louder than blood and honour. Where one's Foes and Allies can be determined by the colour of one's money and alliances. It is the last frontier for capitalism in the post modernism of our global history right here in our town.

A lot of our intellectual people are not being utilised but are sidelined so that crooks and puppets dine in numbers, stealing away the people's wealth under their noses in broad daylight. Here the government has banned all expressions of creative arts and literary voices to erase the evolving culture of the society and the identity of indigeneity. It wants to kill the voices of the people on the streets. Artists are very special in society; they don't just tell stories they reflect our ideas and values as a society. "Traditional arts" is of the past and "Contemporary arts" is of today. Integrated they become part and parcel of who we are and how far we have come.

There are many artists, musicians and crafts people who genuinely want to live a good life but when you kill the voice of the evolving culture, the art on the streets, you deny the culture of the day. The living expression of the society. Our culture is the evolving voice of the people, the living creative expressions. This is a human tragedy, a tale that recites within this citation;

Deep sentiments that are seeping up in time. They will soon blow up. Ethnic violence is brewing and we are but sitting. Don't you know that indigenous hate segregates and deteriorates relations? If we wait too long, we pay the price. So, we've got to stop the blood of our sons spilling on our land. Then again who are we to question the date of what has been and what is to come. For I have lived my life and you too must live yours my dearest granddaughter. My Avia *agira** (though, everyone knows her as our *apeh**, *grandmoth*er in our Bebeli language) seemed to be saying.

Chapter 2

The Greatness of A Rich Man

(From Mila's Notes)

Sisi meri wants me to share my experience as a witness to these social events as a mirror of our time and the leaders who had an impact on our local ethnic indigenous Bebeli tribe.

She said that, "It is better to understand this hate we have, to sink deeper into the past and untangle the threads that have woven our present state of affairs. What better way to say it than the analogy of the song lyrics that goes like this, "When Death Comes Calling". A moral about leadership through the tale of Three Leaders In Our Village, and how it affected our modern world view of our place, the belonging and knowing of our sacred precepts. "

Story 1: The Greatness of A Rich Man

I will begin this tale of morality with the man who was a second cousin of my dear father. He was one of the very few self-made millionaire businessmen of our time since independence. He was very shrewd with his affairs and remained aloof in all his dealings as a man until death came calling swift and plain.

I was told at the time of his "Wok Kastom bilong pinism Wok Bilong Dai Bilong Em*", that with your order from Tegana Pogi your brothers gave a good share whereas many of your sisters did not bring their order and in turn your brothers under paid them. Your order I gave to your brother Daniel and he gave some rice, taro and a big portion of pig. Those who went to junior Harileh like your sister Mamo were not given any pig and only loose rice."

Ha! Such a memory it was that I now recall the vividness of it all. The mere spectacle that fell short to account for the great man and his prestige among our people and that of his peers in our whole land. He was a testament of the potential our people, how they could rise up in life if they set their mind and heart to it. He was feared, liked, despised yet admired for what he represented and that was the lifestyle he was living in both worlds. That of his kinsfolk as a leader and in the new world as a staunch contender. He knew his way in and out of the corridors of power and played the chances that came his way well. The public saw the success, and his family saw the pain and tears. Those countless scars of defeat that carved his way throughout his journey. Indeed, it cost much sacrifice including his loved one's time and his own health but death had become unavoidable at the end.

Like many of his relatives, he was a distant figure. He was closer to my grandfather because his mother was a first cousin to grandfather. By customary obligation he was an uncle to the rich man so grandfather was more often consulted on traditional obligations and rites. He became an important figure in our social landscapes of kinship relationships. At the time of his death, he had been ill for a considerable length of time.

Death had been a long-awaited event in his calendar. As meticulous as he was in his life he planned for the day, with precision and grandeur for a great send off for his own death and the mortuary feast. His family became the actors of the grand finale.

It was a show of wealth and prestige of the deceased's children. Everyone who came to participate in the Wok Kastom did so to witness whether they would match the calibre of his status. For he was one of the pioneers of our modern society elites. A self-made man who made millions by the sweat of his brow. In his later life he led a political life. In retirement, ill and embattled with clans folk wrangling over resource assets and wealth management issues he became resolute to the world.

In death he was venerated to the highest esteem, more so than when he was alive. His casket was escorted with a guard of honour and an entourage of the province elite society. His kin folk flocked to his village causing traffic disruptions along the routes to his official residence. His children put on a great extravaganza - a public ceremony to commemorate their father's memory, but it was a memory of the man he was.

His house was his private refuge and it spoke volumes of the man he was and had become. It was his private abode. He decorated it with all the taste and impressions he had of the worlds within which he mingled and mixed. From the architecture to the artefacts and works he chose; they all rendered the eloquent volume of the man he became.

Just walking around the social landscape of his sacred spaces and it gave an intimate feeling of quiet contemplation.

I am telling you my *pupus*, I have never felt the greatness of awe that I had in the presence of his very absent threshold of living space. You get the feeling that this was a man who had great philosophical ideologies of life. He was a deep thinker that was ingrained by ideologies he held and nurtured within his life time. NO, no I would not lie to the effect that truly this was the greatest man that ever lived in our modern times. I was one of the many eyewitnesses who were privileged to see this spectacle of greatness and grandeur in our doorsteps in our modern times.

The whole show was a signature of his meticulous planning left to his children to execute.

An ambitious discussion of the afterlife he had tried to resolve and reconcile. On the day of his huge power and yet he wanted more as his body declined into the wastage he abhorred. Did death cheat him of life or did he finally find the rest his body had longed for?

Along the way many have developed their own opinion of him crossing paths and rubbing shoulders but he held unto his own views.

I looked at the red carpet that rolled out into the road to create the great entrance for his casket containing his body. People lined the streets to pay their last respects. Dancing troupes were organised according to his instructions. Even the hymns and the details of the hymns to be sung were noted. It was the intricate planning of his final resting place that had me admire the man for stepping out boldly to question death in its face and go in style out of this world.

His children built according to his specifications the mausoleum that would accommodate his casket. It was built in three days by the work men who had been part of his construction company. With tiled mosaics and a foot path leading from the main house he lived in with his children it was a work of wonder and splendour.

People from all walks of life came to see the greatness of the man he was. It was to be the final resting place befitting the man he was. When it was all over, we were left all more bewildered and bemused by the interlude of the architecture of the program. It was like the last farewell he gave in a silent grandeur of the man he was and wanted to be but now he had become committed to our memories of him.

The final act was whether his children would live up to the expectations he had of them. Immediately after the funeral they had the means and their father's guidance to distribute the cultural notes towards their fathers feast the *Wok Kastom bilong pinism wok bilong* day. It was a grand affair, families came and assembled for the great distribution of food. People left with great truck loads carting food packs from the feast.

The following year on the anniversary of his death, only a handful of people returned for the mortuary rites. Those that came only yielded meagre lots of shell money. The grand ideal was starting to rescind into the shadow of the man he was and what he had become. Working in that defeatist state the feast of the rich man was held and came to pass with the legacy of the great man that he had been. This ends the story of the rich indigenous business man whose people were the traditional custodians of Kimbe town in West New Britain Province, Papua New Guinea.

"Wow!, apeh did this really happen?," Mila asked as she checked the recording and continued the tape. "I mean, wow! I could never ever imagine someone from our village becoming that successful. '

"Great men and women are not always born but made my *pupu*. Hard work and smart decisions take you far in this world of hard knocks. It is not always the easy routes that get somewhere but the failures that teach you a lesson in life. Remember that well. That is the moral of this story."

"This person was born to a changing landscape in his time. The colonialists were facing a new tide sweeping across the world as governments were formed and toppled by the mass movement of ideologies of the new world. Imperialism was being replaced by new independent state nations and the indigenous people were now starting to resist colonial administration governance systems."

"In our world, our way of doing things were overlooked and disregarded by the intruders imposing theirs as the best way. We became living mannequins and dolls to this dress up social charade called civil society. It was all so new and affronting but for those adventurous people like our leader here he seized the opportunity to participate in the grand plans of contributing to the new country's vision of a localised government system and public service delivery of services in the province."

"Eventually, receiving a higher technical qualification in his trade before working for some time in the private sector in senior management positions. Thereafter he started his own business before venturing into Politics."

"Throughout his life he had maintained his connections to his kin folks and practiced as well as participated in traditional Wok Kastom practices of the community. Thus, gaining their trust and respect."

"Mind you, he traveled a lot in his work and was exposed to many cultures but had great respect for what he had and where he came from."

"What a story apeh meri," Mila exclaimed in admiration as she checked the recording "*Pupu*, that man took great risks, worked and made tough decisions to get where it took him in his life. He lived his life to the fullest, that is for sure", she added with a faraway look.

Story 2: The Death Of A Village Chief's Widow

Not all leaders were men. We also had our share of many women leaders in our community but not as much as the one that I want you to remember. This is because it is your story by cultural birth right.

I want to tell you a story of your Apeh man's sister, Apeh Veia. Her life story was as grand as the rich man's life but in our own context of grandeur. She was a woman ahead of her time becoming conversant in languages and dishes, customs and fashion trends of different people she came in contact with as hostess and wife to one of our great chiefs and leaders of our time.

She was born in a time of peace but many great changes were happening around her. Her parents were migrant plantation labourers. They were hired to work on the private company estate just next to the now internationally renowned resort and diving spot in the Kimbe Bay area. They were part of the local indigenous band of seasonal workers recruited from the local villages.

A lot of the labour trade movement from overseas had started to stop with the slave abolition movement in the mother land and in Europe. Australia had passed a Bill and that had a great impact on the struggling plantation estates where locals were a difficult lot to hire and coerced to work. Those that were eventually hired like her parents were given incentives such as domestic accommodation to live in. This is how she related her story of being born at the coconut plantation estate at Temara.

She was the second of four children born to her parents. Her mother, Koto was descended of the Bebeli clan of Gaongo and her father was Lolote of the Bakovi tribe of Harileh but they both made their place of residence at Tawaki in Ruango.

They lived there for quite a while during that time, and she had two brothers, her elder brother Linge and her younger brother Joseph. It was at a time after the practice of Black Birding was abolished in Australia and a lot of people were starting to come home from Australia and other parts of the greater Pacific area.

There were good times pupu meri used to recall. A lot of people returned that they thought had gotten lost or died, stories told and sharing of adventures, loved ones gone before and the promises of a new era. The coming dawn in the white man's world.

However, all these happy reunions and good times were suddenly disrupted again. This time great evil was inflicted into the local communities by the invasion of the intruders, more visitors, each with their own agendas and vendettas with each other. After selecting these years pupu Veia now realises that everyone calls that time according to the events that transpired as World War II. The world wars brought a new wave of visitors with a flurry of activities that were unsettling, with conflicting emotional and illogical directions for the local people. During these times, these visitors had a stark difference in appearances. The previous visitors started to leave and go into hiding when these new visitors appeared.

Great commotion, and a lot of despicable things happened as well to the local people which was all confusing and sad at that time. So, they moved back and forth from the higher ground at times and then coming back to the shores, at other times. After some time as the movements started to subside her parents decided to move permanently to Ruango. It was there at the coconut Block of yours called Tawaki that Pupu Veia's youngest brother, your Pupu, was born just after the second world war had ended. It was a time when the great coconut plantation estates were cleared off from the main ***Nuli tanga*** as the government offices started to sprout. A new influx of migrant visitors came and our village people moved away further from it all.

They called that place Kimbe town, the Provincial town of our new Province, West New Britain but to our local people it is and always will be known as "Keveghei".

It was at Tawaki after the birth of her youngest brother Ben that their father died from a short illness. Her mother had barely recovered from giving birth and with a young family she was forced to return to her people after a while. However, her children were brought up by other relatives as was Pupu Veia.

Whilst, in her youth she was given in an exchange marriage between her younger brother Joseph and his wife Lenora, for Lenora's brother Jeff.

As an exchange at traditional marriage, otherwise known as proxy marriages among the Bebeli Bakovi lineages, Pupu Veia became a matriarch after Jeff's death many years later. It was a culmination of years of cultivated leadership by mentoring. Smiling through clenched teeth and duress working through matrimonial challenges and cultural obligations. This was because Jeff was a pioneer amongst his peers and people working in the newly formed government, shifting through the issues with ease and assurances that would ensure that their people would not be bystanders on their own land.

Often he would spend time away from home in long absences when the children were young and then there were times of great upheaval of emotions when people felt aggrieved that he had to settle. He worked through these great challenges as his wife worked in the background keeping their family of growing children, later grandchildren, satisfied and cared for.

In ways the local people now recall her memory as s permanent fixture of her husband's leadership and life as a person, for she was his wife and the mother of his children. This is how I would like to remember her as a leader for our people. The sad irony is that her death had been a very long and harrowing experience. The final closure to the chapter of her life. Here attached is the email I had sent to your mother regarding her death at that time. The micro perspectives of local micro politics among relatives regarding her relationship with us and the *"Mapa"** for us.

Mila's eye witness account

A year now as her final mortuary feast of Pahapipit, the Wok Kastom Bilong Pinism wok is taking place. And it was a solemn affair of last respects and dedication to a deceased.

She had very few visitors given the nature of her illness. The odour of death prevailed upon her death bed as she laid out of sight waiting for the minutes, hours and days to pass. It was a slow and cruel journey lying in silent contemplation being attended to by her only son and his wife.

She had three siblings, all brothers, one deceased. Of the two they both were old and unable to walk up the steep incline of the village to the entrance. Her own daughters had their own families and came intermittently to visit. Now the grandchildren too have grown and have families of their own. Four generations now, from her husband and her union. He was the chief of his people and she too was a woman of noble descent. Theirs was a proxy marriage in traditional Bebeli society.

They had lived as children during the world wars, been witnesses to the colonial administration of West New Britain Province, living through the growth and impact of the commercial agriculture plantations on their lives and their ancestral lands. They were witnesses to the country's national independence and on many occasions been a part of that historical narrative of our country and it's socio-political landscape heritage.

On the last visit our parents had with her, her illness had progressed considerably. She was in a lot of pain and bedridden in the quiet dignity of a great chief's wife. God knows I had cried, Mama wept as she recalled that encounter, "Oh, Mila within my very bones and in my heart, I knew that it was the last time we were speaking to each other. Oh, she was the wife of a Bebeli chief. But in that small window of time, she was only a biological aunt to your Papa, her nephew, and his wife, me."

"Oh my child, it was one of the most heart wrenching moments of encounter your father and I had shared together. Tears threatened to gush out as we bade farewell. We had given her money for her pain tablets as she had requested there and then on her death bed. Saying goodbye was like getting the final blessing. She was the only biological aunt of your Papa and in our culture; and she held the family oral records, annals, oracles and the blessing of an aunt. The burden of truths and the blessings of the wife of a chief and clan leader were released there and then."

"It was a surreal and special moment for both of us. She was dearly fond of Papa and all of her grandchildren and with her famous phrase "love you" uttered to us as we bid her farewell."

"When her husband had passed, the *garamut* had been beaten at low steady beats announcing the passing of a great chief. The *garamut* beaten in a steady tempo resonated throughout the village bemoaning the death of a chief. These death messages are intended for tribe members as a death notice."

"When she had passed on, her in-laws accorded her the respect of a chief's wife. Mourning lamentations were recited with veneration in a night long Vigil around her coffin. They were paying her their last respects. Keening by women, incantations of the death were made by village elders, and were performed in their own indigenous tongue of death. These were newly composed revered notes and odes for and of her accorded to her in death.

Nevertheless, these night vigils were a serious business performed by senior members of the community such as village elders. This was because it involves the delicate act of contrition, commuting with the underworld. The mere business of communicating and conversing with the other realities existence through these lamentations, like personified poetry, are composed to venerate the virtues of leadership a person has summoned during his or her life time. They comprise very sacred and honorific aspects of citizenship within the Bebeli Tribe.

Therefore, they form part of the imagined spaces of immortality that memory accords to heroism and those that are honoured. At times epic elegies or blank verses, they try to emulate a public profile of the deceased's rich journey in life. These are known as the "Kewa" poems. Our people believe that in reciting this poetry for the deceased they submit his or her entry into the underworld, the place of the spirit world. They commit his or her spirit to her or his ancestors through the recital of great warriors and chief in memories within their family linage. They do these so the great heroes in our traditional folklores guide and escort the deceased into the underworld. The place of the living dead.

The singing is a form of communication only sung by traditional poets recounting and reciting the invocations into the death script. Through these lamentations they render the memory of the deceased into the annals of the tribe, her deeds and leadership, while she was alive. There are different chorus parts and the singing continues until dawn where at day break the choir is presented with food and refreshments.

The reciting of these lamentations is arranged by the village elders, the next of kin of the deceased. The poets gather around the coffin and give space for mourners to pay their last respects as they recite the stanzas.

The lead poets start off the undulations and solemn chanting notes of the first lines before pausing, and restarts again with the rest of the chorus who alternate each line with voice inclinations of the gendered parts. This is where I pose the question of validation, confirmation and veracity of eye witness accounts as official narratives. In this particular situation, one lead starts the oratory of deeds as others confirm, endorse and agree with each act and deed of heroism. In Bebeli Ontology the wives of great leaders are also venerated as marriage is a union of clans and forging of alliances. These alliances stand or break at the Pinism Wok Kastom ceremonies these days due to the next generation of leaders' ability to maintain those relationships.

This ceremony I witnessed was sacred and endearing for me as in many ways I was part of the family of the deceased being given this official accord. In her death her memory was cherished and given place among the honoured.

The other important note that needs attention in this recital is the clan structure system in the tribe. In death the deceased's traditional clan songs are sung in mourning chants to wake the deceased clan leaders, deceased relatives and deceased next of kin to the news of her death. This is a courtesy protocol for them to prepare the welcome ceremonial rites for the newly deceased to enter into the afterlife. The indigenous Bebeli people believed in the afterlife and it constitutes one of the pillars of their cosmological worldview of the continuity of their society.

Reciting lamentations, odes and epic statements defines status and leadership of the deceased person in society. It is not only restricted to men but also women who have had an impact on decision making or heroism in life. Papa's late aunt was one of only a few women who has had this accorded to her.

From the outset of Mama's point of view, she said that in looking back at what had transpired she was honoured to have had the privilege to meet her in person. For she was a very special person with a charisma unmatched. We, your parents, had a very privileged opportunity to have had the closure from bidding her farewell.

Papa was blessed to have paid his last respects. He had given her the last request she wanted from him and in return blessed our lives as she left. This very gesture of farewell between her and the both of us remains a significant and important bidding of leadership inheritance and growth of our leadership in our society. That was enough for us. That was why we did not feel the need to attend the Wok Kastom *bilong pinism wok* ceremony when it occurred. At the same time, we are forever grateful for the acknowledgement and gesture of gratitude her family members have given us in the traditional *mapah** that was given to us. That is as much I can say about all this situation.

The irony is in the death notice of her passing how much of a contrast it was to that of her husband's. A silent and quiet acknowledge of her passing was made. More like a closing of the chapter of a life coming to an end.

She had passed in the evening and her close family members called the ambulance over to take her to the main hospital morgue. It was after all these arrangements that a message was sent out to relatives of her passing by a simple phone call from her children and grandchildren. We heard of her passing the next day. So different to that of her husband.

Those death notes emanating from within those drum beats that rose and fell that night conveying the message. Yeah, those tones of regret and sadness.

The quiet incantations of condolences echoing across the land, plains, valleys, hills and beaches. Those heavy beats in long straight strikes rang out into the night, echoing across the plains and valleys with the suspense of the drum rolls. These evocations of death notes and signatures. After it stopped a loud pandemonium of keening broke out. Wailing and loud sobs welcomed the day break. The village folks had only the following greetings with each other, *"lapun man lusim yumi long nite"**

For her case, her children notified us in clear tones of her passing, *"Lapun meri lusim yumi aste nite"*.

Story 3: A Colonial Government Official's Memory Levies

This last story was more of a consequence of the hegemonic intrusion. I wrote this story from Mama's diary of what happened……

Can the years matter in the Bebeli sequence of memories with regards to the tenure of property rights? As much as death is final the transfer of the deceased's property seals that transitional process of metamorphosis between life and death, living reality to that of the other realities.

The rainy season with the wet and cold weather patterns has left its imprints on the copra dryers frame as rust erodes the tin sheet wall. It is a large block and Papa works all by himself to maintain it every week. With the death threats hanging over his life he risks this to ensure his family's income is sustained. Our garden plots are long gone to the overgrown weeds and shrubs that hover above and in between them. It is difficult to *bros** all by himself. It has come to a stage where there are occasional incursions into our block while he is cutting copra by settlers taking advantage of his solo presence. On many occasions he has confronted young men and youths prowling around the block climbing coconut trees, *kapiak,* digging out taro beds without fear or care of what they are doing. It is a very dangerous situation. He hears and sees the presence of Rambo, Back Page and their family flocking to the problem area making garden plots but he still stands bravely ensuring that the property will one day be transferred to you three.

During this stressful period of financial shortage in our family we turned to Nana Wali and Mama Lorna for Kaiymei's noodles and snax biscuits. It is only when Kaiymei gave in to tantrums over food that Papa would make that humiliating task of asking for credit from Nana for those coveted noodles and biscuits.

So, one morning we were surprised to see Papa Nana sitting outside our kitchen on the makeshift *patapata**. He had come to inform Papa that he wanted him to perform the traditional Wok Kastom of demolishing his late father, Pupu Dido's house the coming Saturday.

He informed Papa on a Monday morning. We were informed to bring along some contributions.

The days passed quickly nowadays when we are busy and short of manpower in our labour-intensive lifestyle. We barely have empty hours to our thoughts. There is so much to be done maintaining the house, the blocks and making an income to sustain our lives. I could barely read or paint or even write with the house chores and taking care of Kaiymei. We couldn't even schedule Kaiymei's swimming therapy into our daily program. My flower beds were neglected so many times they became overgrown and littered with all sorts of coloured litter.

I could even see and hear the sneer of the neighbours noticing our adjustment issues. Snide jokes were made about the grass being tall, the dirt strewn foot paths and the mounting laundry on the verandah. I was trying to stay above those community attacks.

When that Saturday arrived, it was just as busy as the other days. So many chores and tasks to complete we were prioritising things to do and getting only the urgent completed. It could be remembered specifically because that was the day that Papa showed Tamana Gelu, the neighbourhood tyrant, where our land boundaries were situated. They had placed some flowers to erect those boundary lines and were both too engrossed in the activity to notice the time. It was only when Papa Baku came to get Papa over to do the customary rites for Pupu Dido's haus that they rushed over to the ceremony.

Mama recalled that they had barely nothing to take to the *Wok Kastom** so she had cooked the tapioca from the block with aibika from our back yard garden. She had cooked breakfast early and was cooking the food for the "*kaniwutu**" ceremony when Papa Baku arrived. Papa sent him back inside so we could carry our food and contribution and follow him to the Wok Kastom* ceremony.

It was a bright sunny day that Saturday morning. The tide was low and the coral beds glistened in the shallow waters as the salty breeze wafted onto the beach shores. A small crowd was already gathering.

Nearby where the popular Kawutu river flowed, a crowd of women were already there doing laundry and bathing. Others sat idly on the dry sand taking long drags of the rolled up local tobacco *"brus*"*.

Little children frolicking, ran and played in the wide-open spaces of the dry beds. Their peals of laughter and yelling rang out in the mid-morning breeze. Barnacles, sea urchins and the bits of seaweeds and corals washed ashore laid bare in the open air, baking in the scorching blaze of the tropical heat. It seemed like a perfect day for this Wok Kastom.

When we went over a crowd had gathered so we sat with Sisi meri No'oh at Nana 's house. While the rest of the crowd sat outside on the beachfront next to the house to be demolished. Pupu Dido's immediate male family members including Rambo, his father and big brother sat under the shade of the trees near the Wok Kastom site. These were the next of kin who were supposed to do this ritual Wok Kastom but as they had neglected it, Nana and his younger brother Papa Baku were performing it. Papa was acting as the nephew of the deceased to perform the sacred rites of cleansing. An act of desecrating his memory into our oral history archives by desecration of the house frames.

I gave our gifts and contribution to the hosts of the Wok Kastom and made ourselves comfortable on one side of Nana's house. More people followed us with their contributions. Clan elders from Pupu Dido's family came and were surprised that the ceremony was to be performed by Papa Nana and Papa Baku. As in many other Wok Kastom ceremonies there were losers and winners.

At this time in the rites, Pupu Dido's family had retained the rights to access and use their family assets without the consent of any of their broader family members. Also, by having Papa do the honours for his memory they had officially recognised Papa to be consulted and informed over Pupu Dido assets and properties. That wrenching of customary rights was publicly declared there and then in front of Rambo and his family.

A small commotion had broken out earlier when guests had arrived and they were trying to identify who would perform the honours of desecrating the house. When Papa was identified Back Page's mother-in- law started wailing and complaining that she was closer to Pupu Dido and she had to be recognised. She and her son, Back Page's son, had plans to move in and control Pupu Dido's assets; her plans were thwarted there and then. She cried out aloud, moaning, and screeching as she rolled and ranted out to Papa Buku and Nana her frustrations and complaints. Inevitably, making a scene in public as her brother Rambo's father hung his head in shame and looked away trying to ignore her.

She ranted on and on in an endless stupor of self-pity until the hosts gave her two pram tambu shell strands to appease her. The immediate families of the deceased were scolded and chided by her, challenging her claims to gaining a pram tambu. She complained that it was supposed to be her son who should be involved in the kastom and not Papa.

We had completed the desecration part of the ceremony were your Sisi man along with Papa Baku and Papa Nana escorted Papa to do the rites. After which the "galesi*" they had prepared for the occasion was put at Papa's feet and I picked it up. It was a bounty that made up for the "mapah"* and "pei"* we didn't receive during the "pinism wok" Wok Kastom ceremony. The items included in this inventory were five sheets of karukah (pendants, woven mat) wanpla ten pram tambu, thirty Kina cash, ten kilograms of a rice in a bag and two bundles of a sixty Kina worth of taro. The whole package was worth around two hundred Kina.

This was a Wok Kastom ceremonial rite that acknowledged and made public the custodians of the deceased estate. Therefore, the ceremony was a political power brokerage between two family units. Although, many people coveted the bounty part of the ceremony they did not know how to stage such ceremony or to come to a stage to reach that level of custodianship.

Realising that we had walked away with the bounty we could feel the resentment ebbing into the crowd, stirring in the whispers and conversations. We had to wait for some people who had to witness the ceremony that delayed the distribution of cooked food for communal eating known as the "*Kaniwutu*" translated in tok pisin as " bung kai". This rite signified the feast of sharing of food and participation of food distribution and eating. In a way it symbolises the sharing of food utensils or coming together of people sharing a family kinship alliance not necessarily specifically or adherent to genealogical or adoption lineage or otherwise.

By the time the food was about to be served it was already going on midday. The sun was in the middle of the sky. Wok Kastoms adhere to strict time conditions where doors to other realities existence and presence are acknowledged. Such acknowledgement ceremonies were installed and deliberated during the morning so food could be eaten at midday and the distribution of the "*kori **" food parcels could be distributed. This is the minor Wok Kastom of the memory rites ceremony of a deceased involving properties and memory levy taxes within the Bebeli Tribe traditional customs. It concluded the Wok Kastom of the deceased property and estate management.

It was midday now and the workers from the sea cucumber farm had already arrived. They were famished and sea blown surf played on their skin in the scorching heat. Whoever we had been waiting for must have arrived because the women at the ceremonial grounds were now serving food. These food dishes were given out in distribution lines to everyone. I was ignored and snubbed in the distribution of dishes by Back Page but your sister Shirley gave me her plate. Papa had gone home to check Kaiymei (whom your sister Mamo was babysitting). He had been snubbed in the food sharing ceremony by Rambo's wife and Back Page.

At the Wok Kastom during the incident involving Back Page's mother in-law's outbursts people whispered out aloud that Back Page and her husband had sold their portion of their family land and now were squatting outside Rambo's father's front yard.

Papa's defense is that he had many good memories listening to his uncle Dido's stories and is entitled to receive his due *Mapah** from his death. After eating, as the Kori* food parcel distribution ceremony continued Papa and I excused ourselves to leave. Heaving our bounty we came home. I gave back one *karukah** to Pupu Nola and had to give some taro too and a packet of biscuit to Mamo when we arrived home.

Mamo told us later that their *Kori** packet was a small portion of pork and packet of one kilogram rice.

The sad thing about the whole affair is that a colonial government officer was the first recruit for the first colonial government from our village in Ruango for the new Provincial government administration at the newly established Kimbe Town. He was the youngest local official working as a translator for the village elders during demarcation of the town and village boundaries. His mother and your Pupu man's mother are biological sisters from a Bebeli clan in Gaongo who married Bakovi men at Ruango.

Much of the original landmarks of the Kimbe town area and the first legalised settlements near the town were translated and noted in agreement through the translation and early note taking skills of this person. His father had originally come from the village of Kulungi but they had to relocate to Ruango soon after the second world war with the other local indigenous plantation workers in Kimbe plantation estates. He had married twice and lived to an old age outliving both of his wives. He has several children and grandchildren by his second wife.

The sad irony was that his life story was not retained nor maintained by his descendants after his death where his eulogy was a blank sheet of the life he lived. His contribution to his people's advancement and the making of Kimbe town went unnoticed and without due respect by his descendants.

In death these three people left a lasting impression of the essence of leadership through the lens of our village people. Our Sisi meri * says their lives are a living testimony of greatness of leadership prestige and power in the prime of their lives. We must translate this greatness into our own lives. One was the philosophy of wealth and to use it to its ends. Whilst, the other was the servant-style service she gave in hospitality, stewardship and life that brought her respect and honour in her old age. Then there is the case of that colonial government official left in the respite of his family members.

Chapter 3

Violent Chants In Kimbe Town

"I had a conversation with a university lecturer today. Mila from Kimbe. And this is what we discussed over lunch. You will find it an interesting read. Perhaps you can read it to Mama and Papa. Much Love, Dubo."

There are violent chants in our Provincial town of Kimbe as we speak. For the town is like the *Achilles' heels in the province's* progressive development plans. In recent months there has been the growing spate of violence. Crime breeds uncontrollably where money floods the local black markets. This triggers inflation in the province to soar. Making it difficult for villagers to afford basic goods in stores and the local fresh fruit and vegetable markets in town. These days Pupu meri listens to the news daily taking stock of the rising lawlessness unfolding in our beautiful town, Kimbe.

From the outset there is a tendency to accuse the growing youth population in town. The young unemployed out of school boys are the main target for this social prejudice and bias that in turn continues to build and extend distrust, that poses neither an ethnic nor economic intervention in its wake. Like waves crashing onto the sand banks our financial issues ebb in tune with the growing influx of migrant population into Kimbe town. Many calls from all corners of the province to address the law-and-order situation continue despite being a development priority for agenda issues.

The issue is not so much the financial capacity but sustainable socio-cultural intervention mechanisms to address the issues with rising crime in the province. To be able to address the situation it needs to have a sociological assessment. There should be provisions in the political and bureaucratic functions of the government on how to intervene, and implement, and enforce.

The problem runs deeper than the transient migrant crime visitors or lack of annual school leaver opportunities in the province. While it has been acknowledged that the province continues to be a transit area for travelers to the islands' region, Provinces in the country drawing trans migration crime syndicates across borders for illegal ventures of trafficking and smuggling illicit drugs and arms trade continue. Even so, Kimbe's problems are inherent and insular, simmering through its generation of indigenous and a vast surging diaspora population where a binary worldview imposes itself on residents' settlement identity. One is either a *waira* (migrant) or *aspeles* (native, indigenous person).

Whilst it is also true that there are school leavers who descend into Kimbe town from their local remote atolls, islands and isolated hamlets to access further tertiary education opportunities, adding to the town's growing population. Not all of them get into criminal activities in Kimbe town.

Block settler descendants, economic migrant workers on contracts, student boarders and family members on visiting holidays have all contributed to this bulging economic burden on Kimbe town's limited resources. In this mix of diverse ethnic groups the increase of the local retail industry's China town presence has added the growing economic class differences to social dynamics in local interactions.

Added to this growing social phenomenon of young people and rising crime in Kimbe town is the evolving youth group identity issues in urban suburbia. It is a situation in which youths in local suburbs have used their familiarity with their own peer groups, where place making and belonging intertwine, merge and submerge into coordinated power struggles of dissident voices in diaspora. Young peoples' temporal spaces of power, security and civic service. In addressing rising crime related issues among young people re-framing, reimagining and unpacking the lens into otherness of young peoples' voices remains invisible and unaccounted in Policy development.

In a similar context, understanding issues of internal security-related threats within the provincial borders and on crime syndicate transnational activities within international maritime boundaries are concerns that are continuously being raised but not further deliberated at the political platform. The increase in crime related activities involving arms, human trafficking and drugs coming into the province are not petty crime activities involving the youth gang cultures of territorial wars, but involve a more organised web of syndicated activities at work. For instance, a recent crime spate involving violence related confrontation with law enforcement, officials concerns over the use of high-powered fire arms indicated accessibility to these weapons by people on the street.

Crime remains a part of Kimbe's social landscape. Whilst rising law and order issues impose upon society, the general public consensus of an idealistic utopian state of no crimes persists.

During recent outbursts on public platforms that denounced the situation of rising law and order, the drastic measures included the calls for incarceration of those involved or suspected of association to the crimes committed. Moreover, in maintaining the imagined state of security, temporal spaces within legislative powers be imposed and enforced. In most instances this concerned the imposition of curfew powers restricting movement of the general public. Inevitably, it subconsciously creates an impression in the public mass media through inference of a near anarchy state of governance on civil society that requires a militarisation zone to ensure the state's governance.

At the outset, the general impression of this drastic political response can be interpreted as symptomatic of a leadership embroiled in corruption. Because basic lifesaving goods and services are not reaching down to the local communities in society where these disgruntled behaviours and disturbances, unattended and neglected segments of civil society create uprisings. In most instances these situations are further exacerbated by the dire resources available in attending to crime related injuries and incurring costs in the crime zones. As a consequence, highlighting how this vicious cycle of civil society discontent can lead to disturbances of a larger scale. This can trigger civil uprising where with limited resources to attend to public safety becomes issues of national internal security.

Therefore, in constructing disaster management planning issues with internal security protocols, a guide for best practices and policy for emergency services must be seriously considered. After all, trans national crime related activities are national issues from an international threat to our national governance.

To understand the dynamics of rising law and order situations in West New Britain Province, one of the fastest growing economic provinces in the country, it is important to reframe the lens to the 'otherness' of young people's narratives on rising law and order challenges in recent years. The rising urban population of young people is one segment of the society whose voices are just as important towards understanding and constructing intervention strategies to the situation. One of their major concerns is the ongoing issue of human rights infringements, committed against young people where juvenile justice within the context of indigenous and transitional justice remains obscure and invisible for them as citizens of the country in the province.

With the continuous loss of lives and properties, the financial costs on businesses both public and private has been enormous. The unfortunate demise of technocratic wrangling and cultural alienation. Plus insular Policy Planning in urban town development h a s   created issues that contribute to the current tide of law-and-order problems in the province. To such an extent it is apt and evident to assert that the political governance in our province renders a shameless human rights record on its own citizens.

Obviously, many critics see the Provincial curfew imposed in Kimbe in 2023 as another window dressing by the government to stop reprisal of the Lakemata killings incident. This was a knee jerk temporary reaction to soften tension in Kimbe town. The public outcry over the killings were attributed to the fact that the mass prison killings had occurred in a prison in a secure institution facility.

A day later police shot on defenseless mothers and young people protesting the killings in a public gathering in full view of the public. The law enforcement officials press statements defended the police shoot-out as a reaction to restore public safety as opportunists went on rampage amongst the protestors. There was a media blackout imposed on the relatives and associates of the prisoners killed in the correctional institution and on those who were hurt participating in the protests.

Prior to these incidents there were no effective arbitration avenues within the Provincial government administration for civil society on the one hand, against state institutions and agency employees and the state itself. The nonexistent mechanisms for human rights abuses, created this civil unrest yet the mass media propaganda blamed the vulnerable and less empowered in society. Our youths and the women.

The reactive measures adopted by the government established provincial desks representing the youth and women as per the provincial organisation structure of bureaucratic governance. All these changes were being implemented during the temporal space of a state of emergency curfew months imposed in Kimbe. As these political instruments of technocrats wrangled through their land-grabbing agendas, civil disturbances and natural disasters continued unabated.

Living through these times of uncertainty is like walking through the valley of death.

Let me draw your attention to some of these target patrols on the streets on many of our neighbourhood curbs and sidewalks, streets and bus stops. Public safety is the slogan yet in many instances, these parades carry agendas of their own in the face of our ignorance.

These slow beats of patrols are working on the naive innocence of our sons.

Steeped in plantocratic epistemologies of racial hate now manifested into ethnic economic class wars. From the colonial past to intimidate the indigene people into second class citizens on their own ancestral lands. The colour games of monetised culture of underworld economic rules; creating a tide of segregated privileges and benefits where Equality once ruled, that ideal of utopia.

Now to think that the Baby rascals' phenomena is a familiar place to carve out a story. It's walking through the valley of death that rings a bell of atonement. An awakening to see the targeted prejudice on our young people. Black pearls in our midst are a rare find. So much for justice on our land.

Chapter 4

The Nightmare

"I didn't sleep well last night Dubo." Mama complains this morning. She continues…..

It's these apparitions, more like nightmares that visit me in my waking hours in the studio listening to Phil Collins and trying to make sense of my place here in the village. Since you and Dula have left there is barely a sense of welcome of my presence here except that of tolerance. Now I am only re thinking my staying here in the village and how it has affected my career as a professional visual artist. Please tell me what you think of this recurring dream.

In the dark muddy bush track a woman is carrying a pile of firewood on her head. Slung down on her back is a bilum string bag laden with garden food. She is returning home from the garden. Too tired, weak and weary to have a conversation but in her head, there is a conversation going on affirming her status as person.

"I'm A Survivor", she thinks. "And I rose above all those scanty squalour attitudes yeah, my shanty backdrops of town life. With all these empty dreams of a drifter chasing dreams for a better tomorrow. Yeah, and I rose above all that social stigma, street seller mama working to feed my family. After all, life knows no class because it's fate that divides every person but whether you are rich men or poor men we all die one day. We will all one day meet our Maker."

Yet my mother 's folks always reminded us kids that it was never like this before. Nobody knows what exactly happened in specific details or what happened next or how our world came into being except through the tale of the box that holds evil that unleashes the power of grave consequences. Now time has seized me in my mind there are stories that need to be passed on to the next generation. They need to move on. Towards the next chapter and the next generation who will need them to find their place in this world.

After all, is it not the maze that we are fitted inside in the precepts of human awakenings.

It is something to do with resilience. Trying to be here when all else presses you down.

From the distance, there is an echo somewhere where the voice resonates with this statement:

> *We are the last of the original people but we are still half caste. Not the full blood original descent of the great Bebeli Tribe who once lived here. Yet their stories are our stories our ancestral rights to belonging and connecting to our surroundings and the living precepts of the ecological web that exists here. Our village Ruango is an old abode of many centuries and generations that passed through our shores and the forests. They are the keepers of the oracles that our people use to predict the future and hold the thoughts of our very existence. Moreover, it is our living and learning centre of life, and living and believing of our existence. This is our tale of how our land was taken from us as a people and the political genocide of our people in our own provincial history by the hegemonic intrusion and institutions of colonisation on our traditional landscape.*

I had woken up that night soaked in my own perspiration. I tried sitting up after drinking a glass of water but soon sleep came back to embrace me back to its bosom. Now in this new dream I was transported back somewhere, somehow in time long past during our ancestors' time. Memories surpassed life to a space where neither life or its essence could take specific shape. A juncture in continuum temporarily displaced or rather interrupted then disrupted by a cosmic explosion.

Oh God, a destructive sensation of calamities beyond human comprehensive notion or imagination had transpired burning my consciousness to the core. I had never felt such damning pain all over my body.

I opened my eyes into the blaring bright sun light streaming into the windows drenched again in my sweat. Papa had woken up earlier to catch up with the traffic to sell the copra he had made to pay for the allowance this month.

Oh Dubo, wish you were here to discuss this nightmare. I don't know what this means. Is this a bad omen. For the first time in my life, I feel so lost without you kids in the house.

Papa is so involved in taking care of the plantation to send your monthly allowance so I am left with this domestic space devoid of humans. I'm counting the holidays until your return.

I wish I could change the tone of this email but to be honest it's still here. What I mean to say is that the nightmares are still here. It is one of those irrepressible ones in recent days. This time I actually told your Papa about it but he was so busy he said he would go have a think about it while he was at the block and come back with his interpretation. It has been three days since we talked and he has never raised the subject again.

I am too afraid to ask him since he is so busy these days he barely sits up at dinner before hitting the sack at night. He has been doing all the labour-intensive tasks and he is not getting any younger. I worry about his health these days; the strain of the financial burden is taking its toll on him. Please pray for us as we do for you.

It is as if we are reaching that peak in which one is soaked up in the terror of the night as in the "Dream of creation for your contemplation".

A voice like rushing waters cascading down the ravines sharp edges where the waterfalls fall on big boulders at its feet. The tale was intense and booming with the immense weight of certainty imprinting its impression unto me.

Once upon a time many years ago something happened to change the entire course of human history. It was called the *Foroga* in my Korafe language because I don't know what the Bebeli would say. Anyway, it was more like the day of reckoning.

It was a night like any other night on that fateful day they say. A time where sleep had been deep and restful. Dreams were sweet and blissful of all things merry and fun. A place in a time where all the weary people nestled down on their beds in fitful subdued rest as life was meant and practiced for a merry and fulfilling routine of adventurous living. So, in the evenings there was a comforting presence of relaxation until that time the darkness came. Oh, how the moon hung low indeed it did.

Huh!

It was a tragedy from which we have never fully recovered let alone fully grasped within the limited world view of humanity. Who would have even told us or forewarned us of this coming doom. There that night the grave travesty was soon to strike while our people slept. They were as dead as the living night. It was right after the monsoonal season had passed and the land with its unrelenting chill had descended upon the evening air. The warmth of the dry season had not even surged, heaving like an envelope of warmth in the night like now. People long for this evening weather where the moonlight was bright and gay as the stories told around fire places. The cherished indulgent past times of great harvest seasons.

Ha!

These were the days when young lovers met under the frangipani trees courting. Garamut beats reverberate in solemn notes of unity restrained and cautious as families bonded around their hearths. Loyal and devoted to each other whilst love and respect glued and held everyone together. It holds memories that warm our hearts of good and happy times with people who matter the most.

On that particular night, something in the deep vale of human deceit descended down unto the homes of every family: men, women and child. There and then planting the wisps of doubt in each person's heart. It was the child of the imps who strive to deceive. It came crawling in mists of descending dusk swirling through their consciousness to cause anxiety in their depths of logic.

No one can say why and what made them come but they came anyway. It was however sad to note that despite having many wise men who were forewarned of the coming tragedy only a few had actually prepared for it. These were the people who had actually and continuously taught the village people to be cautious and watchful of the vengeance of the night watcher and its magic.

Many generations passed and this forewarning became a mythical oracle to the present generation. After all, who among their living memory had had a life of hardship and strife? Here in this time so many things were taken for granted as food was plentiful, good laughter was infectious, and friendship was valued. To them life was an evolving right to be lived not to be cherished but used abundantly.

So now of all nights as they took in deep slumber both creatures and mankind, they knew no bitter truths that lurk in shadows. Alas, how their lives would be changed into a bitter end as disharmony weaved and threaded a path into their hearts and consciousness.

Seasons came and went for as long as they remembered, or so they thought lying in their beds. All round them nature bloomed and flourished uneventfully. Life and goodwill reigned unceasingly.

That night human beings' behaviours underwent a scripted social change. A metamorphosis in social cognitive reaction both emotional and psychological. Thus, altering their worldview of their place in society. They had worked hard and long till day break spreading and altering their homes. Soon day break came as swift and delicate.

When people awoke and broke their fast, they felt light headed like something was missing. Each person started to brood whilst children started to cry out in slight irritation. Angry words were spoken, eyes leered towards women as much as men as laziness clung onto their limbs making chores become a burden of necessity.

It was as if they all woke up to chaos everywhere. The world of happiness they once knew had descended into madness. From a place where couples loved and children grew in grace in an adorned paradise, homes disintegrated. The serpent and his minions went on a rampage wrecking homes and lives. It was all in the mind, people playing mind games where Aphrodite sat solemn with a bewitching stare and Cupid was let loose to play. Pandora ran amok through the centuries spreading its crazy and endless curiosity among all mankind. All the while at its tip of the tail and wings, vile imps of all kinds sailed past. A legion of tempest terror had begun its mark of war on happiness and the innocence of humanity.

The voice said that there are different versions on how this situation was later recognised and resolved. However, residual imprints continued to rear its face in our social landscapes often.

I had woken up refreshed and more confident of myself than my previous experience of nightmares. This was what my mother would call a building dream to nurture my own self. A reawakening with my inner sense of connection to my landscape. An experience where I would have to say to myself *"Kokoi Fuyo."*

Oh Mama, had I not realised how much she depended on me? I read with such sorrow how my absence had affected her emotional and mental state. Now reading through your emails I see the emptiness that has left you with such a despondent state.

Chapter 5

Black Widow's Tears

"In the past month", your email continues…..

"I have lived within the enclosure of my own feelings trying to come to terms with this empty nest you left behind with your departures. My version differs from your dad's version as parents but the traditional Mokorua language poetry lamentations of Kaita is from a woman's lens. So, my version seems justified to be here for you to view.

Mine is not only chaotic and violent but also yielded to the sadness of one in mourning like lamentations of the dead. Like a widow's lamentations I recite to you:

Kaita

How often was it that her mother-in-law dared to look at her in the face.

Her eyes piercing and boring into the widow's. Searching and imploring the widow to confide in her.

But she sat there very still as the cold of the night for the burning ache of despair engulfed her, and as tears slid down in an endless rage. After all, she was a woman sunk in defeat. Death had robbed her of the most valuable wealth she had ever owned. It was the salt of bitterness that stung so annoyingly as she cried for yesterday's memories, tomorrow's promises and today's emptiness.

She was in fact mourning for the companionship that ceased when the closest person to her soul passed on. It was a sorrow that countered the greater loss of the quality of life the woman she had shared with her late husband.

It was bitter and cruel because they both had dreams for the road ahead for their family. Now as a single mother she has to walk that journey alone. In the depth of her anguish is the void he had left in her life. Now that he's gone they have both parted onto their different routes.

Her dear husband and friend was a sorrow consuming her every waking moment.

Kaita is an exclamation of longing as much as sorrow. It expresses the void that comes to the homestead on family members. A lethargic spell on all the occupants of the house making them feel powerless and helpless in its face.

I know I taught you the Kaita Lamentations as you were growing up. Now it stands like a replica of your past. A bilum you left here at home when you went away. For me it is the feeling of diaspora and now it grows deeper in old age as a reminder of the beauty of life that once was.

Like the dance of the purple violet they were engulfed into a realm of depleting energy I saw another one of those traditional Maemae* performances today. It reminded me of this unfinished business of this poem. Now in this translation of the lamentations of the battered wife social justice theme note.

**These Fading Purple Violets where did they come from?
They all wondered out loud.**
It is as if the dance of death in the guise of Silhouettes under the moonlight. Behind closed doors whose windows of the house have covers drawn closed. Here, there the crashing and thrashing continues long and dull bluntness reverberating all around from them.

After the commotion a lone figure huddles in the corner snivelling and weeping silently.

Fading violets over the horizon she cradles the hurt in her heart. In the quietness, her thoughts surface and confront her as her children lie fast asleep in innocent slumber. Where moments past they all shared the anguish and fear in the raving rage of the one so dear. It was the scars and bruises in streaks of blue and black lines.

Oh yes it is just a plain shame lame blame heaped on love and these baskets of flames of anger in the family home has maimed frames of her role as someone's wife, lover, mother, sister or aunt.

Battered all the same at those times until we all in our modern society. Say ENOUGH, IS ENOUGH!

These are the shades of the wet Season. After all, the wet season becomes a metaphor of the lessons nature bestows on our lives.

Dark clouds loom in the distance with their dull deep hues to dampen our moods. It is like digging a large lump of soil to prepare a new garden.

A personal investment towards sustenance then prosperity. But herein the air is sinking and closing into a tight fist where you are and the light all around you starts to dim and rescind into an abyss. Here now you start to hear the sky quiver and growl with groaning rumble as flashes of lightening cracks in fury its streaks of flashing light. Acting like a drama freak show the actors detest attention.

Then and there as the roll of thunder gains momentum heaven's tears gush out in drizzle and then in bucket loads and crash out in flood such is the storm that brews from the shore of time. This is how you can tell when pride will sink into the depth of Ignorance.

Just as there are different shades of wet and dry seasons contained therein the life of this mama's voice.

Ps Note: With all the intimate partner violence incidents reported in the media these days I am saddened that there are some commentators who think it is a traditional practice in our Melanesian culture....It is deplorable even to suggest. So, where our Wok Kastoms through engendered space respects and values the woman as an integral and valuable asset to the continuity of one's community and society. Hope you can relate this perception t o your intellectual community at university.

I am thinking of compiling these notes into a working novel about life in the Pacific Islands from an indigenous women lens. You know like a life experiencing the joys and sorrows of a diaspora woman living in a village and living through its micro political landscapes and micro perceptions.

Like a personal journal of snap shots of village life with the following content structures of which I intend to use the analogy of a bilum as reference to the feminine baggage of independence whose values are rooted back home in Melanesian identity values.

The string bag back home is a work about intergenerational relationships of women in Papua New Guinea through cultural lens of Melanesian society. It explores the socio-political challenges, hopes and aspirations of women trying to cope with changes in their roles and responsibilities as mothers and her daughters.

Whatever, the truth or the consequences of both their decisions on their lives and their relationship is their lifeline to each other and their own destinies. Derived from an on-going family drama about living in a village on a small island community in the Pacific the drama starts to unfold when the family had to make adjustments after their eldest daughter leaves home to pursue a science degree in one of the country's premier universities. Based on the mother's emails to her daughter regarding the Melanesian version of "keeping up appearances with the Jones" the novel explores middle income class snobbery cliché of village cosmopolitan lifestyle Pacific Islands.

The working theme is on the ethnography of shame through a Melanesian lens where the story's development re-imagines the ethnography of shame in a close-knit extended family whose Kinship and domesticity values are changing. It unravels and untangles the psychological reaction to coping with shame by some characters. Whilst with others we experience how shame as a cognitive reaction becomes an emotional experience; with others it is an act of piety for intellectual humility. This illustrates how agencies of change affect the essence and values of the concept of shame.

The emphasis here is that shame is a phenomenon involving social constructions of self where personal values are concerned. Therefore, I am interested in rendering the experience of how new values change attitudes towards each other and how one reacts to others in the context of shame. A profiling of the act of shame through a multi-facet lens on the characters reaction towards consumerism and how it affects personal judgements on others. How much change has affected our values of relationships and social status within our community?

In a more subtle way, it raises identity issues between the characters of the story where each one tries to start their family history to justify their place in the community and access to property rights. The description of village here describes an indigenous community living their subsistence way of life and whose members are related to each other.

Since, a Melanesian village comprises a close-knit extended family living in a hamlet together where phrases like "wanpla haus line" having genealogical ties from a recent matriarch or patriarch in the hamlet. In this instance, the people in this story have a link to a family patriarch as a great grandfather of the main character.

The title in itself is a metaphor of place, family values and the cultural experience evoked by the personal renderings of a mother missing her child. It uses this local identity as a bridge to cope with change happening in society. I wrote this novel as a conversation in the context of a mother giving news snippets of home to her daughter in her emails citing "since you left" as a narrative anchor. This is to emphasise that a lot has happened to her family and a lot of adjustments were being made as a result of these. Thus, it is a story of a mother learning to live without her eldest daughter's presence citing time as an essence of life, not to be dictated. Using the analogy of running water it cascades at a pace undeterred on its own course traversing a path forging forward and onwards unaffected by the passing scenery and their dramas. It is a narrative of human experience from a mother's gaze about being transported to a social space of public leadership in lieu of her child's achievements in society.

Whilst, on the other hand, there is the kind of shame too that renders respect. This is the kind of shame our people practice in the village ceremonies of "Wok Kastoms" acts. It originates from acts of intellectual humility. It is associated to the phenomenon of Awakening and the act of or pertaining to "on becoming". It is not condescending nor denigrating but rather articulates empathy towards others.

Between these two poles of opposite forms of shame, there is a grey area of articulation between the lines. An intersection in that we as indigenous people have to learn to read if we want to participate in the wider capitalistic market driven environment of our modern society and its institutional structures.

Here I am interested in weaving through a narrative about connections involving human relationships during changes. How they unravel social masks as in the statement "people wear masks like *Biriris*.*" *(the masked man)*. Over time people unpack and unravel their true self through little indiscretions that consequently unveil their real intentions.

Social dramas in Melanesian societies as described in this novel represent a new cultural dimension of our changing social attitude involving dynamics of power plays so subtle and silent as invisible junctures of our local environment. When it becomes an ongoing attitude and occurrence, we become complacent and complacency creates stifling inertia, a clutter in our progression to our life goals. This is what I wanted to represent about life as the story unfolds as per the mother's statement, "at first I thought I did not realise the shifty body languages but as days passed and the frequency of their attitude made me realise on what end of the pole they were. Either they were our friends or our enemies. It began to dawn unto me, unravelling and peeling off slowly before our eyes the masks people wear on their faces when they see us. This is a result of trying to make sense through the mists of what was happening with us."

I want to discuss how human language within different social landscapes around us provide new insights to "how we use our limited "value" resources in valuing each other".

To ascertain the statement,"what type of things we use in our lives self-identifies us from others". Moreover, i t is expressed here in the mother's statement.....

"A whole experience for us as a family was like opening a new chapter of a novel in progress. New awakenings of our own life values, strengths and weaknesses. It is like being thrust into a social realm to find our own footing, adjustments and allowances to function as a family. It was a multi-dimensional experience and had multi-faceted implications on our lives. While it brought us joy minced with sorrow etched on a blanket of love it opened up our eyes to how success divides loyalties of people in our circles of influence. It is like traveling on a new journey of evolving paradigm shifts in human relationships with those around us and whom we meet. In unpacking those layers of human trust issues at times surreal and uncomfortable we become more resilient and more alert about our own circumstances."

That is what I am thinking of these days. Perhaps we may look towards the golden sun. Yes, that promise that says,

Oh,

the tide of the golden sun is where streams once flowed in shimmering light formed the backdrops of a nation's dawn. It is where the curtains of hope flutter in the scenes' promises, where bridges high on visions shine were built. Their initial intent is to hold the future seeds our forefathers told and, in that time, suburban dreams begun.

Now these streets are deep where they were once mere roads. Now they hold back alleys behind the busy traffic flows. This is where little hamlets of shanty huts loom housing. Where people of diverse ethnicity live and conduct business by the rules of class and greed. Where hunger pangs drive the survival needs and each person to his or her need.

Pockets of trust on Issues of hush become the guiding norm of security out of the ghettos.

Dignity is a price we pay someday. Yet the concoction of weeds, pills and booze divide the lures so much that it becomes too risky a game to play, for one to ask, what is pride in another man's shoes? After all, city jungles' silent codes of survival includes: street talks, little lords party hordes to shame and muck but then again there's no pride in a no win situation.

Now and then, sometimes, a city chase with gun fire in the broad daylight rush. Someone's son, somebody's brother. Whose husband is going to be picked up tonight? Clean bill call the shots, Pull strings under the table and foot the bill for them big boys.... Dirty games on double dips, white collar crime, Social crimes and Moral lies. How do we define such acts?

Where is decency in society where doll girls flaunt their wares in hotel foyers

Money man fortnight rush with sweet lies

where pillows dance and Silent thoughts.

they transpire and conspire till dawn.

where dust of reality shakes off

until the future and the twilight streaks of the breaking day sets forth.

Money divides and classifies people here

Yet we all share the same view towards the golden sun.

Good night.

Chapter 6

The Matrimonial Verse

Everyone in the village desperately wants to change their narratives and this often causes tension as I have experienced and hereby recite.

They say life is a journey that one travels. In that journey one has to meet fate in order to meet destiny with all the seasons in stride. The triumphs and losses are woven into the script and we become actors on that stage. Where ever and whatever may come along the route of chance.

In every culture and every race on this earth we all have a story to tell to pass on an insight like a guide to steer the next generation. In the wide Pacific Ocean, our people hold onto those stories in many languages in different ways so we can sustain our connections to each other and our place.

The abode of our living remains alive and well in our memories. This is one of those stories and it is the story that is sung as an ode to our lineage to honour our continuity. It is a traditional rite performed only by women elders of a clan. It is a lone voice that echoes like a river that Meanders through time with all the drama, tears and triumphs that brought us back to our homestead again.

This therefore is our story from my grandmother's time in the recent past of colonial administration and governance period to my daughter's present time. Like a fabric woven by women in rich layered tapestry, so are our lives.

Here on the island the ocean can be seen in all its magnificence and threatening power over humanity by all who live within its reach. Nothing has changed its course until now. In our present state of conquering ourselves and the spaces we dwell and move within. In the Pacific blue, we the women of our clan, continue to bear the fruits of our actions.

I am the voice of conscience that moves in family trees where old age grips me by the arm of truth and makes me realise some old truths about life.

Like many newly married, I too want so much of this to be the highlight of my life. In the long term plan, I want it to work. It is a verse that sings to me now as I look with renewed strength towards the future.

Even Papa now spends a few minutes a day to talk and chat so I feel that I have now found my footing and look forward to welcoming you back home soon.

Mila and Dubo I found this old poem about a couple growing old together it so very much reflects your Papa and my life these days.

The Promise Of Holy Matrimony
For in the Holy Matrimony sacrament we as couple make our vow that symbolises that Together we promise to travel this journey of life through the deep vale where dim light casts shadows on our path but we will stand side by side.

Sifting through the hurt and tears in between the pandemonium I will find your voice is my promise.

For you are too close to my heart. Forever leading me to you even oceans cannot stand between us. And when dusk shall come calling, I don't know how ready I will be because I cannot Imagine life without you. After all those years of tears, laughter and happiness in our lives.

For me then to What is life and what purpose can I have in life without the one person whom I cannot comprehend life without: you?

My brief interlude has been interrupted by the surging wave of sensations washing over me. It was sucking all the air out of me.

Pushing me with such great force back unto the bed. I laid there in my own sweat listening to my heart beats thumping against my chest. I had never felt so alone, helpless and defeated than there at that moment of time. My throat was parched dry and brittle as the seconds ticked away into minutes and hours. I had no sense of time except remembering the scream in my head.

Hey! Hang on ! Stop!

As the first morning birds started to chirp, I felt the weight of this presence that weighed me down get lifted. The air around me shifted as the morning rays started their descent.

I felt my limbs were free again it was as if whatever had trapped me had left me. The presence had left with its gloomy dominance over us. After that dark encounter Mama had said that the dark presence whatever or whoever it was never returned again. It reminded her of someone. The very persona of a wife basher. She remembers because of her poetry about the subject and having being around victims of intimate partner violence, of domestic violence cases.

The man who beats his wife in the village is treated worse than a street dog because our culture treats women with respect according to her roles and status in the community. So, the odour of death in domestic violence is a strange phenomenon for us villagers. Unless this is a premonition of something or rather the awakening of something sinister.

Then again, to understand one's actions you have to look back at where they have come from. Firstly, it's one of those days of ramblings again. Secondly, on another subject one evening around dinner time we experienced a paranormal activity of a **dwarf encounter. By** the way, your sister Kaiymei and I now use your bedroom because your brother Dido is afraid of the room and prefers to sleeps on the library lounge. His fear has been fueled by a paranormal activity that happened to us in the living room one evening. It was a nice afternoon when the warm blaze of the sun reclines with its brilliant gallery of hues and we had settled down for dinner.

Papa as usual had prepared dinner and sweat glistened on his face as he put the plate in front of me. Next to our plate was Kaiymei's. Kaiymei as usual crawled over to the side of the plate ready to pick at the food on her plate as I pulled it away from her. It was hot in the small bowl of hers, with visible whiffs of hot air rising out of it. It was a typical village staple meal of coconut creamed taro kongkong in turmeric accompanied by fresh ferns and spices. I sat in the corridor leading to the bedroom where my papers were situated. All neatly strewn on the floor in piles of three heaps at the back of me. The door of the corridor to the bedrooms was pushed back to the wall, lodged loosely by my other leg as I sat.

Papa sat down next to me facing me and close to Kaiymei so he could feed her. He was flushed from the torrent of activity as he finally took his seat. Kaiymei and I waited for him, calmly watching him and waiting for him to cool down so we could all eat together. Flushed and his body bathed in sweat, he sat looking endearingly at the both us. He said the table Grace before feeding Kaiymei the first spoon of mash before he took one of taro to his mouth. I followed his lead in eating when I felt the dizzying unsteady gaze before me. It was as if the earth had a blurry wavy motion taking place where my head was pushed towards Papa's face. For a miniscule split second a strange sensation overwhelmed my physical being.

I stared at Papa in shock because I felt this pushing of our head towards each other. It was an unruly push where I saw Papa's face grimace at this split-second motion before I instinctively turned around to my back to see what had pushed my head. Then I saw an outline of a human figure so short, well built in a stocky stout frame rushing out from the back of the corridors door frame I had lodged back with my legs. That was when I jumped up in shock and screamed out aloud in a terrified squeal pointing into the middle room looking back at Papa.

" *Aiyo! wanpla dwarf yah,* " *I screamed.*

"Em sot olsem same height olsem displa TV sidaun long stand. Gragra blo em olsem blo Kaiymei taim em ino save comb".

He was a short and stocky built male dwarf or a young youth perhaps already married. He was being cheeky and had a height the same with the TV set on the small stand on which our TV is perched. Papa got up and ran into the room and thrashed through the stuff inside the room but the little man had since vanished into thin air. We returned to our meal and tried to retain some sense of normal conversation from this brief interruption of our interlude of thoughts and family meal time.

Throughout this encounter Kaiymei laid down silently listening to our conversation without uttering a single word nor even making her moans and whimpering mumbles. This was a when I realised that we had met a very cheeky character of a young and mischief person trying to disrupt our family time together.

Ever since I had lived in Ruango I have heard stories about the dwarves but this was my first actual eye witness account with one of them. Given the many comments of the elders of the village that our house is situated at the spot where the dwarves once used to live some centuries ago. It also proved the same opinion of people that dwarves were cheeky perverts with voyeurism indulgences over humans. It explained that and made me realise that there were numerous occasions in which there would be skirmishes and petty arguments triggered by these creatures at the expense of our family life in our community here. So these tales that cited the colony settlement of these creatures in our neighbourhood had some merit after all.

We finished the meal still shaken by our encounter. By night fall the place cooled and we were more relaxed. Dido came home for dinner. We excitedly recounted the experience to him. Dido was not around when this incident took place and had gotten quite a fright thinking about it. He became vigilant and alert within the rooms when he is at home ever since.

Take note here that the old people in the village say that our village sits on the site of a huge dwarf camp. The local people believe that there are all types of people either dwarves, cyborgs, humans, fairies and imps of the forests that pass through the land. However, the more human activity through a growing human population, the more it is destroying this inter relationship between us. The destruction of large forest areas is killing many of our neighbours' habitats. To an extent where the dwarves who were once creatures of oblivious existence now walk boldly in front of us and amongst us with mischievous glints.

To this day there are not many who can still recall the stories of the other human creatures of the forest nor have we maintained those existing relationships.

When the government headquarters was established in the newly named Kimbe town the colonisers wiped away our indigenous rights as a people and a tribe, scattering us to the surrounding fringes and we, the clans that were present, chose to stay while others went further into the hinter lands. Never mind our tongue or social structures, they imposed upon us that their ways were far better and superior compared to ours.

They remained on every site, nook and cranny within sight taking away our rights of association and cultural landmarks, making their domination our abomination exact. No never mind the fact that our land was never at any stage, "Terra nullius" they pawned their way with inducements to accept their gifts of payment. Nor did they comprehend that the land was never really ours alone but part of a living ecological system of social relationships that they had now severed by their ignorance and cultural insensitivities.

This was a sad and annihilating experience because other indigenous people in the province also participated in this hegemonic intrusion on our land and called it development. Today we call it Land Grabbing in the context of indigenous human rights. They participated and took away the Bebeli peoples' land to build a province headquarters without acknowledgement for local customary land owners as traditional custodians; nor as an official tribe. These people are not just the visible indigenous villagers and their kin but all the inherent colonies of human settlement within the indigenous cultural social landscapes within their ontological and cosmological ecological systems.

Sometime after your father and I decided to work on our language revitalisation program we noticed there was tramping and thrashing on our roof top and ceiling. It was a loud entourage of marauding rodents traversing through our derelict dilapidated house frames at night. Might not have been rats but a group of dwarfs strutting around in our house. This was a possibility we did not rule out though as it brought on a vulgar awareness that it preyed upon our indecency, our private spaces and violating our clothes and underwear. These creatures were playing havoc in our lives and with each other to fulfil their appetites. I am convinced that their presence absorbs the positive energy of success in our environment. Taking it away.

In that great conquest of land grabbing, throughout history our people have had to face many challenges of scientific research and experience where they have been subject to studies done by outsiders on them. Throughout which great myths and fantasies started to filter through their precepts of accepted beliefs systems.

Chapter 7

Reminisce of the Reiki Dance

As dusk descends stretching out its arms over the land, and sinking sun rays over the sea, the skies disappear like the curtains of the day drawing to a close in our little hamlet at Tegana Pogi. The kundu drum beats reverberate with a slow rhythmic tempo calling the dancers to the dancing grounds. It drowns out the distant sounds of traffic into intermittent far away echoes; and nocturnal creatures emerge vibrating and coaxing in the cold breeze.

This steady flow of cool air displaces the distinct scent of rotting fruits spruced with the smell of mown lawn.

Close by, the peals of laughter and light banter of little children's voices walking in small groups to the meeting place may be heard. They move towards their grandparent's voices singing in harmonious tunes the ancient tongue of the Bakovi people. They sing of events long gone and buried in memories of the past.

Whilst the bigger boys imitate paddling strokes with actual paddles, singing beside them in the outer rows are young girls and older women swaying their grass skirts in unison. The facial expressions show grief, anxiety and resolute determination which adds more character to the performance. The male dancers' bold warrior like decisive tones are intensified by the women's dismay and mournful cries.

The accompaniments recreate the melodramatic climax of the overall performanc

Alternatively, some will read this traditional dance choreography as more of a silent cultural resistance towards outsiders and their hegemonic intrusion on indigenous lives. Afterall, *Reiki* describes ruptures in society that lead to discontinuities in our narratives of the past. Our history.

The dance within its own performance is an evocative commentary of lived memories that echo from the dead about what happened in the past. It re-enacts this oral history with emotional intensity and understanding of a particular occasion. It has a spiritual element of psychological trauma that lingers into the present reality. It is like experiencing the phenomenon of Awakening the past, today. A communal act of remembering. Through the windows of imagination and the emotions of the past, history becomes a critical analysis, drawn from memory and expressed in a dramatic dance story.

This dance is like a door that opens to the previous realities of time, place and obliviates time's pauses and raises the memories that are held in recess, now untangled. They surge with glowing freshness, fast and filled with the intensity of a flaming, scorching itch, to relate the tale, drama, tragedy and woes.

This is how all of life's memories of significant events are passed onto the next generation. Our history books in dance.

In Bebeli cosmology, the dance reactivates memory as an invaluable vessel between the past and present reality wherein, the phenomenology and philosophy of society's experiences are fundamental to the safe continuity of the peoples indigeneity and identity.

In other words, the dance *Reiki* is a communal lens through which the arrival of the church missionaries is often remembered. As an invasion, intrusion and disruption on their social landscapes, entrenched and embedded into the emotive language employed. In dancing the *Reiki*, you begin to realise how the old and new ideas merge and recreate a reflective space of diverging values and aspirations of a people living in transitional temporal landscapes.

This local experience has been a multi-dimensional exposure for all of us involved.

In dancing *the Reiki*, I want to discuss here what has been in the realm of Christianity and specifically in relation to spiritual warfare.

These days, the *Reiki* dances become a living reminder for our people in the village of the intrusion of Christianity on indigenous lives. It is one of the many living repositories of oral histories and archival knowledge of the Bakovi people that have since then remained as a silent resistance to the religious hegemonic intrusion of the church on our shores.

These early invasions, intrusions, and imposition of Christianity onto our local people has, over time, erased a lot of our traditional oral histories embedded and entrenched in many of our local traditional dance choreography and lyrics such as the *Reiki* dance. Histories, so that when you look closely at the dance, it portrays a long sea voyage, illustrating the connection with other Pacific Islands indigenous communities that have deep cultural connections to the sea. It resonates. We are after all sharing and connected by one ocean.

Another aspect of traditional engendered spatial values expressed in the dance is women's political and functional roles in military warfare as human shields for the men. This confirms early European contact records of indigenous communities in the Pacific Islands where women were the go-between for the visitors and the men in their tribes.

Last night, like the many nights before, we felt the emotional intensity of the dancers especially, those of the male dancers circum-navigating the sea. Little girls like Mita have been consistent with their commitment to the rehearsals. Under the moonlight their voices rise and fall in tempo with the drum beats, voices from the grave reminding us of the unspoken deeds that were buried in time. To other members of the rival movements, dancing the Reiki and its subsequent preparations for the public performance re- creates an analogy of the Bible story of Joshua and the Israelites blowing the horns outside the tall walls of the city of Jericho. They did the Jericho March and the walls came tumbling down.

Like those that scorn western hegemony's impact on indigenous people there are some in the village who regard the act of commemorating and glorifying the intrusion of the Christian church establishment with disdain. This is because it implies that the indigenous people were uncultured without intellect and organised socio-political structures as a society until the church's arrival.

They are in a faction of the new science group who view *Reiki* dance drama as a meta language form of oral narrative about a distressing incident in the past whose memory is re-enacted. It represents an historical trauma. More precisely, traumatic events that have happened and the impacts they had and how the trauma is carried from one generation to the next signifies these indigenous people as victims of progress. They argue that the lyrics are sung in old Bola language and express emotive feelings of dismay in remembering.

Thus, retrieving the past with its emotional intensity and expressions of shock as creativity through time and generations. Again, and again.

It is so beautiful out here in the village wish you were here to see it.

Pupu Koch, Ray and Pupu Lo'oh with their sisters and families have been rehearsing it faithfully since then. In the initial stages of the rehearsals the floor plan of the dancers had the little Sunday school children out in the fore front. While the bigger boys imitate the paddling strokes with paddles singing beside the outer rows of young girls and older women swaying their grass skirts in unison. As already mentioned, it is the facial expressions showing grief, anxiety and resolute determination that adds character to the performance of the male dancers. Memory reenacted.

A researcher, John Bodley in his nineteen seventy-five publication describes it as, "traumatic events that have happened and the impacts they had and how the trauma is carried from one generation to the next signifies these indigenous people as victims of progress".

Our old Bola language is perfect to express the emotive feelings of dismay from remembering. It more or less retrieves the past with its emotional intensity and expressions of shock as through time and generations as expressed by indigenous Māori anthropologist, Lily George in her theory of Historical Trauma studies has noted.

Some of these impositions include Christianity and its theological philosophy on indigene historical experiences and narratives by early European contact on their way of life. While there are those who will read through the lens of mysticism and the feminists' construction of identity values and platforms. However, it is the objectives and underlying motives of commemorating this event that intrigues me as an indigenous person.

In our Bebeli cosmology, the dance reactivates memory as an invaluable vessel between the past and present reality wherein, the phenomenology and philosophy of society's experiences are fundamental to the continuity of the indigenous people indigeneity and identity. In other words, the dance *Reiki* is a **communal** lens through which the arrival of the church agents, the missionaries, are often remembered. As much as an invasion, intrusion and disruption on their social landscapes entrenched and embedded therein in the emotive language it employs.

The *Reiki* dance traditional choreography dramatises an interesting traditional Performance Art that needs to be unpacked, untangled and re-framed into the Province's official historical narratives. It is a traditional cultural practice whose traditional knowledge and structural processes are endangered by rapid erasure imposed by disruptions of its agencies and vessels of transmissions.

One way this challenge can be addressed is through teaching the dance in inter- generational community activities and spaces such as the Tangana Pogi dance rehearsals each year. The other most urgent need is to encourage more scholarship and research into this traditional heritage knowledge among our young people to pursue liberal arts and humanity courses in tertiary education institutions in our country and abroad. In that way, we will develop interests in research into our tradition heritage cultures both material and in knowledge systems. After all, culture is an evolving aspect of society that needs to be harnessed in a way that is sustainable, reflective and informative throughout many generations from the present. Since it is an integral aspect of nation building that binds not segregates our people in our diversity. Moreover, acknowledge and support the evolving process of cultural diversity through intervention strategies to ensure sustainable art practice incentives that encourage the development of the local entrepreneur and the cooperatives that initiate and install collecting agencies to safe guard intellectual property rights of the arts and artists.

On the other hand, traditional sacred performance arts practices should be encouraged as micro enterprises in the village level to reach their full potential as cultural heritage materials and knowledge systems that need sustainable development and management practices guidelines. The long-term goal is for the installation of a village museum and cultural centre here.

My point and that of Pupu meri is that in dancing the *Reiki* you begin to realise how the old and new ideas merge in recreating a local reflective space of diverging values and aspirations of a people living in transition. The dance within its own performance is an evocation of living memories that echo from the dead about what happened in the past. It re-enacts this oral history with emotional intensity and understanding of that particular occasion. It has a spiritual element of psychological trauma that has lingered to the present reality. It was like waking up to the phenomenon of Awakening through the windows of my imagination and the emotions of the past.

Oh Dubo!, when I first saw the dance and it is a traditional dance drama choreography I was truly mesmerized by its entire performance. The Reiki dance is about a long voyage over the sea. You can feel the emotional intensity of the women of the male dancers circum-navigating the sea vessel. Little girls like Mita have been consistent with their commitment to the rehearsals. Under the moonlight their voices rise and fall in tempo of the drum beats like voices in the grave reminding us of the unspoken deeds that were and buried in time.

This is how our village rehearsed for the missionary's arrival at our village next to Kimbe town.

This sentiment is born from our legacy of the Pacific slave trade in various stages of the intrusion. These conquering of our spaces, values and minds. So to sing and dance Reiki in various motifs we divulge in our oral history of ruptures within our social narratives as a people in society. That is why as much as it is a dance of commemorating an event it is a dark heritage that can be applied to the episodic tales of the time of the great long-lasting drought on the island, New Britain in Papua New Guinea.

Part 2

Sorara Da Kiki Saida Erena

(Micro Perspectives of Identity)

Chapter 8

The Carping Back Queen

Did you know Dubo, that Mama's chief antagonist among the lot has been Mama Watermelon. Another close neighbour, she lives next to the Gelus who are also our neighbours.

When you ask me how to describe her there is a concoction of emotional intensity that comes into play in my mind. How can one put into words the melting broth of episodic encounters into a character of a person? To me Mama's stories of their encounters are like water drops that pass through your grasp in the nick of time. So, the most arresting features are summed up here in this profile.

Watermelon is a typical gossipy village house wife trying to keep up appearances in our neighbourhood. Our little village cosmopolitan lifestyle creates its own version of the Melanesians version of *"keeping up appearances with the Jones suburban middle-class syndrome"*. In other words, you could say that the impact of capitalism on our indigenous lifestyle in the Pacific can be best defined from our family encounters with Watermelon.

Our experience is described here *"She wants to epitomise and copycat everything you have become. She wants to promote her children at every opportunity that they are smart and as clever as you with that up your nose social attitude".*

This is Mama's version of how things would start to fizz out between the two of them from the cordial and mutual respect to an all-out confrontational conversation before they part from each other ...

An example of one of my encounters with her soon after you left was a day she had come across me weeding in my flower garden. The conversation sort of went in this direction:

Me: Hey Susa morning (greet her upon seeing her carry her bucket to their main water pump).

Watermelon : Oh morning sister .Yu ino pilai yu clean up na mipla sample ino yet.

Me: Omo, mi bisi long bik girl ya na olgeta haus wok silip faol stap.Nau tasol mi laik stretim displa flawa garden.

Watermelon: Em yah, noken tok mipla too yah.Mamo(Watermelon's eldest daughter) too yah em mekim gut tasol tisa blo em yah, Missus Jay tok larim em stap hia long ples mekim grade nine long wanem Kimbe Secondary school . E yah ol mangi ino save mekim gud.

At that point Mama recalls t h a t, her stomach did a flip and she really wished she could do an eyeball roll there and then. She just could not help herself to cringe at those words with such egoistic vanity. All Mama could think was, how dumb does she think we are? I mean, is she ignorant of fact that Kimbe Secondary school   science graduates had been the biggest number by far in recent years in the province to receive tertiary institutions offers for the new academic year's enrolments?

There and then, Mama felt very sure in her heart that Watermelon was among that list of people she resolved to run away from and avoid interaction with.

She complained that Watermelon's attitude towards her was like a combatant on the field of sophisticated idiot empty-drum. The behaviour of someone with low self-esteem from the emancipated heritage background who use carping as a way of righting wrongs. It belongs to people who are uncultured and cannot articulate their views well. They have this false impression that by talking down on people as a form of justification but it only hurts them more as being aggressive as an aggressor. Often becoming a hot head that people avoid in social networking.

Mama says that in many ways she is always on the combative mode when she interacts with Watermelon.

In looking at all this cast I am reminded of the Bible verse in Ephesians chapter six about the whole Armour of God. Indeed, the spiritual battle is true and real. In all our days we are drawn into a spiritual battle field. "We need to be alert to the devil's playground." Mama has since resolved

You know Caitlin, the thing about Mama is that she likes to state that the English playwright Shakespeare was right, we are all actors on the stage playing roles from our own script. Until the good creator and master calls us all home someday. Whether it is a tragedy, a farce or satire it draws us all into the unfolding drama where all our lives are somehow connected to each other by some form, idea or connection. Either way we travel down the same pathway in our own time in this village.

On the other hand, the African American author, Toni Morrison had aptly cited that there is no such thing as growing old discussing it in her novel Jazz. We just adapt to life challenges we face along the journey. Our people in our own indigenous way of framing life's destiny attribute change as another milestone in the continuity of life that extends the societal life span of our oral history. We sing and dance, distribute wealth assets and food to acknowledge these personal experiences. They are narratives to our memories that we create about our lived lives. This spiritual battle field is a playground our lives are affected and impacted. Again, I am further intrigued: is it me or am I deserving of the treatment of mimicry Watermelon is giving me? She had resolved.

She had told me soon after that she was going to seriously go into novena to find out "how and why Watermelon and Kina Gelu pick on me. I mean Mila seriously", she added, "why do they behave the way they do?"

Since Caitlin left Mama has been complaining that Watermelon has been mimicking our actions as if we are the optimum level of family success. Such as putting the preschool video music on loud speaker for the baby, but the baby is oblivious to her mother's intent, nor is she at the scale of milestones to receive the banter. It is a mild form of child abuse.

"I mean Mila for goodness' sake" Mama had gritted her teeth at Watermelon. "Who does she think she is and what does she want to prove?"

After that incident she kept away from meeting Watermelon. Days turned into weeks and the months she avoided her until one fateful afternoon it became unavoidable because an incident had happened and no one else in the neighbourhood was around so she sought assistance from Watermelon. It was about five months after the first encounter. This is her version of what had transpired there and then.

"There were two girls who had appeared on our presence while we were talking so Watermelon tells me that they are Bett's sister."

"Remember Macy and Ruth?" she says.

"Well, they both have big teaching jobs in Port Moresby" she tells me with a smirk of self-importance.

"Oh, really?" I say trying to comprehend what she says. Without thinking I ask, and "Sarah?"

It is when she pauses hesitates and exclaims "she is doing girls work experience at Mosa?".

This response gives away the phony setup in her mind so I stop there. I bid my farewell and leave realising this woman is a foe not a friend.

She is striving to make herself look important because my presence intimidates her. Firstly, like Papa always says," *Madi there are no other good professions in the office other than being a teacher.*" Secondly, a university degree in a recognised premier institution is more highly regarded than a college short course certificate. Thirdly, you cannot get a good job in Port Moresby coming from the backwater of Kimbe with a certificate from a little known business college.

I am pissed off walking away thinking to myself, "*what a nerve of the woman, I am not a village woman secluded from the city. I do zoom conferences with colleagues around the world and participate in international discussion panels every year. Just because I don't dress up and show off they think I am dim witted like them. Time to keep off their pavement for a while.*"

What an ignorant world Kina Gelu and Watermelon live in.

Then who am I to question their intellect as mere mortals that they are. In opening my eyes to these issues what will I do with this information and awareness of my situation? So the statement "everyone was born with an intellect to distinguish right and wrong, to move on in life and interact with others. However, it is death that will separate us; intelligence and wealth are what makes life animated. This is how the beautiful words of the Psalms twenty-three are favoured by many:

> *The Lord is my shepherd; I shall not want. He makes me to lie down in green pictures; He leads me beside the still waters. He restores my soul; He leads me in the paths of righteousness for His name's sake. Yea, though I walk through the valley of the*

shadow of death, I will fear no evil; for you are with me; your rod and staff, they comfort me. You prepare a table before me in the presence of my enemies; You anoint my head with oil; My cup runs over. Surely goodness and mercy shall follow me all the days of my life; and I will dwell in the house of the Lord forever.

When it comes to Watermelon the combative attack is subtle and spliced into a friendly banter before I even realise it's too late. This type of spiritual attack is decisive and premeditated before they are even executed. It is the mind of a highly conceited enemy waiting for my down fall. Realising this is more painful, because it makes me feel so dejected and alone like a sheep among wolves. All around me they stand and watch waiting for my daughter Caitlin's (Dubo) fall from grace; ganging up on me with their sneering and side remarks. It is very lonely standing out here in the public scrutiny. This limelight is too bright for me to look at the road. My enemies are many and friends so few.

So, this is how women like me felt when they left home marrying a man of foreign land and culture. They had to adapt to the new lifestyle, cultures and standards imposed upon them by the society. With understanding partners, they flourished but for the unfortunate ones it became prison like entrapment on earth. It is not something new, it is part of the human civilisations that lived throughout the generations. We are all living that same narrative in our own time and circumstances. In a way, it explains how the love, respect and bond Ruth had developed for Naomi in the Old Testament was very special given the different changes that confronted their lives. But their loyalty endured, persevered and in turn opened doors for them in the most difficult times. It is in extreme conditions that we are able to shine when we hold onto our faith and stand against the rough long road. So Caitlin's journey has become all of us, our journey in trying to achieve a dream God had predestined for our family.

Chapter 9

Mama's Antagonists, The Praise The Lord Alleluia Couple

Mama says that the most psychologically challenging trials of late in the economic class wars is those periods where she feels like she is living in a state of emotional and mental torture in the antagonistic presence of Mista and Missus Missionary.

Just being in their very presence is like having to be constantly receiving acidic doses of sarcasm rubs on our consciousness. They think so highly of themselves in the neighbourhood putting up that big act of being sophisticated Christians with money, and show in the neighbourhood, to sneer at our poverty. Their material wealth they like to flaunt at every opportunity and chance.

Just a mere mention of their names evokes a bad taste on Mama's emotional state. Here is how she describes her encounters with them…..

"When I was growing up, I read an interesting novel about a teenage son and his mother. Although, it was from a migrant person with a diaspora lens on trying to find his place in society, the story left a huge impression on me about a mother's influence on her child's life. This is because it had the voice of a young person trying to fit into society. A young teenage boy trying to find his way around his social landscape and who needed his mother's guidance and support. However, his mother, a migrant settler, was also testing out the cultural protocols and social rules in her new neighbourhood. So in the end, the mother starts to realise her son needed her as much as she needed him to find their way around society's rules and expectations."

I was fond of that story back then in the nineteen nineties where the grassroots women mobilisation and empowerment was at its height in Papua New Guinea urban towns and cities.

These days I see the same scenario at play in our society and more often call it the " *Look At Me*" committees. These are middle class suburban women in our local communities who want to be in all the village committees. They want to be seen so much, to the extent of neglecting their parental roles and duties to their children and husbands. Their upper-class snobbery stains their fellowship to the extent that it makes a serial killer become more like a saint compared to their pious vanity. They act as if by being in every conceivable committee it will buy them a seat in heaven. Except that, what they give off in vibes is the scent of insecurities of a mother who is unable to understand her kids and trying to be a saint abroad to avoid resolving the issues at home. These are people who think their position and stature will excuse their children's behaviour. In many instances, they are the classic case of how "*baby rascals*[9]" are starting to sprout.

Many of the children thrill seekers causing armed robbery delivery runs on hire come from middle class income homes. At other times, they are at the lower ranks of street pushers for their suburb's drug dealers and merchants. More often, they tend to do these activities because of parental neglect. In most instances, they are often a child crying out for parental attention. Whilst, for a lot of them, the parents of these children often think that they can use money to buy off their family's wrongs and short comings so they try to solve the issues by high level snobbery to those who see through their lies and excuses.

It reaffirms the notion that money can be a great deceiver in the climate of economic class differences, social dynamics and wars in the micro political structures of a village setting. Where people are undergoing change at all levels of society. This reaffirms the notion that we have a lot of social climbers clamouring for attention in the corridors of power and scrolling through the social graces of insanity

---

9 Teenage criminals

like never before. It's like becoming a crazy modern pose: *Missus boss meri syndrome.*

Then there's the wannabes who come to steal the show of fantasy-lives using trendy chic diva methods in broad daylight like the Filipina drama they've become addicted to on pay TV. These women of the ghettos with little imagination think highly of themselves and towards others are social Labradors panting for public attention that masks the obvious assertion that we are so busy looking at the child we do not look at the overall picture of where he or she is coming from. What kind of mothering dynamics does he or she come from at home to trigger these childish behaviours?

The other point is the issue of relational dynamics in the neighbourhood. The village on ancestral lands poses the kinship affinity identity values foremost for all. Whilst, in the plantation estates or institution barracks there are the levels of modern wantok kinship alliances of childhood mates, school buddies and work mates, and their group dynamics. Each group has its own sub culture that influences your world view of where your loyalty lies. The level of loyalty and value of relationships upon where you were raised in the country's economic class structures is an important determinant of how you react to change and contribute to national identity issues. To an extent, where there is a cautionary gaze, you would need to pause and note that not everyone will see through your lens of what happened in the Port Moresby riots because the class walls aren't the same, either way you are standing in the country. Different people experience different coping strategies and a mother's influence affects our worldview of choices in our alliances.

Why have we stopped looking at the colour blindness of greed in our modern society?

It's people like these who engage in silent clamouring for social validation at all costs, by all means, leaving behind a trail of destruction in their wake. I used to ignore it before but as I am growing older it starts to become an annoying nag. Thus, I don't want to be all nice and put up with plastic courtesy. Why do people want to hold the lies to their breasts and shun the painful truth before their face?

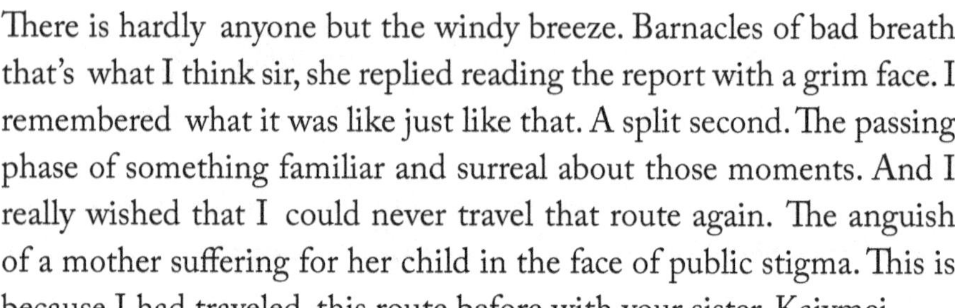

There is hardly anyone but the windy breeze. Barnacles of bad breath that's what I think sir, she replied reading the report with a grim face. I remembered what it was like just like that. A split second. The passing phase of something familiar and surreal about those moments. And I really wished that I could never travel that route again. The anguish of a mother suffering for her child in the face of public stigma. This is because I had traveled this route before with your sister, Kaiymei.

God, no one knows those tears I've cried. Every month I held her in my arms trying to hear the good news rather than that devastating tone calculating the head increase. It was always so devastating.

Ha! but they would not know the difference, would they? They have been so stuck up about it all. It was as if they chewed gossip like savoury dishes trying to find fault in our lives just to justify her condition. The sneers and jeers they threw at me as a mother with special needs child was their favourite past time. It is not something you would confide to anyone but it was something f o r w h i c h you grew a thick skin j u s t to live. Survive as best as you could in the circumstances. I pulled away from our community church activities because of their attitude. I have no regrets about it because it was unbearable living through their sarcasm. These Holy wars of mockery.

There are drunkards raving their heads off again tonight. The music from their boom box is at high volume. Trashy high-strung Metallica and they are yelling and shouting when singing in lyrics. This banter continues trying to provoke us all into the wild ravings of a scorned woman.

Someone with low self-esteem needing attention to justify her very existence. Like death bells of folly being rung endlessly. Now the pious feel for their own face value looking down on things to please their subconscious self and all. Huh ha!, the village economic class wars are being played out again before us.

Those agonising nights, when Mama told of how she tossed and turned as the sweet aroma of brewed coffee whiffed through the wire mesh windows. God knows how my stomach growled and grunted in emptiness as hunger pangs burnt my insides, crying myself to sleep. Those were the nights when God was far away and the reality was the pit of hell.

In retrospect, I can attest and attribute this couple to the attitude of Pharisees in the Bible who were at clash-point with Jesus Christ in the new testament bible stories. Whilst putting up a big public show they have since become alienated from their own responsibility as parents to their children giving them gadgets instead of their time and attention. Now none of their kids seem to want to go to school. They have lost brownie points too in our community by avoiding assistance in paying school fees for relatives. However, what really hurts is when they take a swipe at all those who are struggling to make ends meet in our neighbourhood.

I cried when your sister Destiny's mum recounted Destiny's story of how they had tricked her during Christmas holidays. They made her believe their empty promises and lies to assist in her school fees. But when the new school had commenced, they got transferred out of Kimbe town without contacting her or even fulfilling their promises to help her. God knows how antagonising it is living next door to them and to witness their blasphemous religion.

I am disgusted watching them pray loudly in public displays to assert their holy appearance but their actions speak otherwise. Lately we have been at the brunt of their evil and tyrannical behaviour. Like hell on earth their tormenting attitude burns deep into our bones. Gyrating their powerless wealth of moral ignorance over our struggles as a family. I find it hard to reason how parents who act so holy and righteous, have no control over their children's insensitivity. For instance, they are constantly blasting their radios and television volumes to the maximum level polluting their intellectual upbringing in an act of flaunting of their materialistic possessions to the neighbours.

Sadly, I am amazed that they do not realise how they are documenting reels of their public menace and ignorance on Christian virtues.

They have been too busy to notice the insanity of it all. Building empires of social exclusiveness over others' communal spaces. All this whilst they do not know how to teach their own children the important things in life: like respect, honesty, hard work and sincerity. And in the dire circumstances of others, having empathy for them.

They treat their kids like heavenly beings and make ours like primitives from Mars because they eat chicken for dinner every week. I hate these transitional periods when they come to the village with attitudes so high and mighty like the fallen God's of opportunity on a promotional road show of their stupidity.

The mother sits in every community committee full of self-importance but practices complacency to act as the devil's advocate in our neighbourhood when her children are concerned. We sit and sleep, listening to their petty decisions over others' lives that enables their attitude to look down on others in the neighbourhood and the community. These condescending behaviours separates them from us in our attitude to life.

Unlike Vavi Nina, I am the one that wants to run away from their presence of wastage. They are just as wicked as the Gelus but the difference is that they use the church as a front window in their game of sophistication.

Chapter 10

Other Antagonists

Worst of which is now during this time of the year at Easter that Mama tells me that she is reminded of the piety of Job in the old testament. His faith in God was gravely tested through the many tragedies that he encountered in his life. He went through the most compelling intellectual journey of humility.

Sometimes it could also mean trying to make sense out of circumstances within one's own life. A personal process of unpacking tolerance through perseverance as part of human growth. It is as important as much as that story of the Israelites trying to build the destroyed city of Jerusalem through the Prophet Nehemiah 's version in the Book of Nehemiah in the old testament. Here the emphasis is in the process of unwrapping the human character of oppressive resistance towards those who are working towards a long-term goal. He describes the emotional and psychological reaction to strife between opposite factions and the strategies they employed in their stance. Here again the Bebeli semblance is within resilience of one's own family lineage in weaving survival through alliances.

It is a virtue of leadership to be patient and practice intellectual humility and endurance through submission to a person of seniority whether by age or group status.

In her recent email to me, I am glad that Mama has an anchor now in my sister Kaiymei. When times are tough and the feelings of despondency try to discourage her she says that it is our sister Kaiymei that becomes the silent remedy that pulls her out of the black clouds. These are the days where Kaiymei makes her look at the brighter side of life. Oh, Caitlin it has been an insightful time looking over at the way people have treated Mama.

Tough is not even an acceptable adverb I could think when reading these stories. Has my departure caused a purge to occur? A temporary glitch in human relationships? My heart bleeds at this news because I never expected these reactions towards my family.

Yes, I can see and realise that they have more work than they had ever did now that there was no one to help in the chores.

"More often these days we crawl with our weary bodies to bed at night slipping into a deep slumber. Our overworked bodies have lost their lustrous streak and supple glean and are now riddled with wrinkles from too much exposure to the scorching sunlight. At the same time, our bodies have shrunk into hardened skeletal frames walking like the living dead all due to lack of adequate rest. Every day we scramble to make ends meet in this very expensive living-standard. We seem to be eternally swimming against the rough current of life here."

On the other hand, at a different level, Mama had some shocking fresh insights about her foes and friends.

"Our lives are like a new awakening. Realising that people we respected as friends wear masks before us and reveal their true voices when our circumstances change. In the midst of our troubles their rear heads appear when their expectations are not met."

"My sister Amima is one of them", she says. "She had bluntly asked, "what's so different about your daughter? My daughter studied the same courses in year twelve with your daughter but how come yours has more opportunities than mine?""

"I was simply too stunned to reply", Mama reported. I was also shocked at this encounter.

"When you had left, you had been the envy of everyone. But behind the smiling faces and the jovial well wishes they were waiting for you to fail. Praying evil onto your good fortunes. We were the greater fool thinking they were our friends. They were not the people we thought so highly of. Their true nature was revealed after you met your demise. This was of course after the long wait they had waiting for your return to the village following your demise at semester one enrolment. You surprised everyone when you left for Rabaul instead of coming home and peoples' reactions to your movements opened our eyes and ears to the under currents in people conversing with us."

"I remember my sister Amima's house is a gathering place for all the nambis boys and they were the source of my ongoing misery considering your situation. Issues you faced have become public broadcasts in the village. In recent weeks this has brought out a lot of people's hidden feelings towards you and us as a family."

"Let me give you an example of such an encounter. I had just brushed off that defensive and cautious stance of walking past Back Page and Rambo. The incident soon after those public snubs further exacerbated my anxiety for the day. Yet the good thing was it increased my weariness of reading people's body language towards me. I have been passing them in Morekea town and feeling that air of indifference coming from them. A predatory consciousness and a silent look of mirth from Rambo and his family as much as Back Page and her family. They walk on with a hunched frame trying to shield their naked intent. Like a dog with a bone to pick they shuffle their legs in front of them to shift the dust under the shoes of their feet."

"A rumour ran wild on the local grapevine that you were coming home and dad was too poor to buy your ticket home. This from the Vavi's hamlet at nambis peles. Too many people we thought were our friends and trusted, then revealed their real colours. Nobody wanted to speak to us or know us by then and we became outcasts hitting rock bottom. From intellectual elites we soon became economic low-class citizens due to your demise. People wanted to believe rumours instead of hearing the truth. It opened my eyes to their intentions. All these bush vines either exaggerate or distort information to suit their own needs. Gossips and rumours feed on misinformation and in turn become subject of character assassination of individuals without credible evidence. This was what had seemed to have been the motive but somehow died down.

This incident illustrates how the growing diaspora population in our urban centres have become estranged from their kin folks at home. Then become alienated from the land and rights within.

"Now more than ever, we were able to see through people's intentions. Those so called "*wannabes*" flaunting their money carelessly in front of us making us feel like social low casts in society. The chief amongst them being the Gelus. This is because the next day after your departure Tamana Gelu and his wife went to great lengths to show off their kids going to school. They made loud noises grunting, fussing and ranting on so the neighbours could see how diligent as parents they were about education. It was like a plastic puppet show entertaining us all. Kina Gelu all made up like a China doll marching up and down the road for all to see her new status. She was oblivious to all the snide comments and jeering the public was directing to her. To the Gelus, keeping up appearances meant flaunting the little plastic acts to be recognised. At night they drunk and raved on about their plans of conceited pride for the whole world to hear. Like modern day fools they live next door to us looking down on us because our daughter made it to university. They were becoming competitive in areas they could use to attack us, like our yard, trying to create strife where none existed. Like the right to inheritance of properties such as land."

"Their attitude reminds me of the statement, "their green eyes of envy ogling over our success with sunken grace." Thus, they get competitive with envy stained with jealousy. Running a course in unchartered waters without knowing how they will benefit from this destination; just piggybacking on someone else path out of miff and ignorance."

"It was as if they were spiked by the imps of envy, greed and conceited pride who were using this couple to throw spears at us in our vulnerable emotional state. They were using emotional tactics to sabotage our plans.

These little disturbances were trying to get our attention and divert our attention from looking at the big picture. On these occasions we were like Job in the bible who had gone through his own issues of strife in his life to understand his own relationship between God and himself within the contextual application of Christian intellectual humility. At the most extreme ends of servitude, I could relate to the old testament Prophet Jeremiah and his own issues of tolerance in his vocation as his own family life spiralled into chaotic and tragic consequences. It was like traveling through a social tolerance battlefield unfolding itself in our lives."

"My daughter, as the days turn to weeks in our lives, we unravelled certain truths about people. Either their intentions, motives or the inner intent they had been harbouring and pretending to be good all this time. Here in our village the ongoing saga of the devil's playing field continues. After all, isn't it all coming into reality that time in itself is a better test of character?"

"Watermelon's husband said they had no shame. It was so disgusting living next to them, he told Papa one time. He had been complaining about their behaviour off-handedly in a conversation after you had left when the toxic situation started to vaporize into a mist in our neighbourhood."

"In a similar instance, do you know how it feels when you come across people and they scramble to run away from you?"

"I have noticed this occurrence lately. People avoiding me like a social pest. It happened almost the day after the Vavi's elder sister Vavi Nina scrambling to run into the expatriate people's fenced yard when I strolled by the three ways lane."

"Apparently, she had not seen me coming until it was too late. She had been having a long intimate discussion over the iron fence with some people there. She had worn a long jersey collar shirt pulled over her calves. The shorts she wore were of blue faded colour jeans trimmed off in mid thighs. She had worn a light make-up on her face and whiffs of perfume oozed from where she stood."

"Whatever the conversation was about she seemed all preoccupied and intensely engrossed in the surroundings until I passed her. Then, panic stricken, with a warped face she gripped one of her small brother's hands, dragging him with her. The poor child jumped up in shock turning back to look at me and I was in as much shock as he was."

"Clearly she had not expected to see me nor wanted in any way to interact with me."

"Vavi Nina had left the village for Talasea before Christmas soon after her year ten examinations, with one of her friends. She had not returned after the new school year began. Her mother had forced her father to send word for her to return. I had not seen her until now. However, whatever feelings I had to greet her disappeared with her reaction that day. Ever since that day I think she has been hiding from me and Papa. She must be ashamed of not making it further in her education. It is so uncanny the way her mind works. We are not the school inspectors of her life. Despite her father's best efforts to assist her to further her education she has shown no interest but to go to market with food produce. She engages in drinking sprees with Back Page and women in the village neighbourhood."

"Papa has complained on numerous occasions when he witnessed her, and her sisters, verbally abusing their parents with swearing and vulgar remarks in public. I had just now got my dose of her psychological reaction to my presence. A taste of real self."

"Remember Na' aman the Roman soldier in the bible who was a high-ranking officer with respect in the empire but whose life was judged by his physical appearance. Of all his personal and career achievements it was his skin disease that was his most grievous affliction in life. Social affliction is a human condition that can be attributed to lack of achievement in educational pursuit as witnessed here in this incident. A situation in which Vavi deliberately avoids interaction with us."

Chapter 11

Dubo's Kokoi

"Wake up you people!

We cannot afford to lose touch with our blood lines. Oh, I grieve for us.

Grasping for the seams of seeming truth we have drawn dark shades that hover rather than stand as the backdrop because values change with time but blood in our veins is the same. Since heritage is defined, you are reminded not to let outsiders preach you down. In other words, know the roots from which you came because these dark shades remain."

A woman tosses in bed. Beads of sweat trickle down her face where it soaks through the threadbare cotton night dress she wears. In her dreams the words boom into her head. She can see the future and unlike others the promise of new beginnings, dismissing climate change and the pandemic crisis as previews to a larger threat against humanity. For the subject of ecocide remains an enigma and a political rhetoric of humanity's task of stewardship gone wrong.

It is a story to be told like a collage etched within are all pieces of pleasures, triumphs and losses as pain and laughter like stitches in hard knocks. Those unforgettable lessons inscribed through those tears of wonder a beautiful patchwork emerges and shines through. Here today with a verse to share so that in time together I will gather as addition, the adder that I am.

When s child is born and given a name his or her Kokoi
is acknowledged and remains until death separates them.
Parents use this phrase in place-making and introduce

this phrase as an important aspect of human integration and inter- relationship to the physical spaces of where one lives and interacts with others. It is an important tool for the conceptual frame of spiritual knowing and awareness to nature and its way of working. In the age of internet technology and outside influences, changes and shifting priorities in life, the concept and knowledge of how the Kokoi functions in our life has been erased in our social values and contemporary cultures. However, the applications are there.

Therefore, I am exploring this phenomenon within our culture through a scientific community of cyborgs creatures, the time warp space and time travel experience, labyrinths, matrix and continuum value systems and structures of functions. In reusing the Melanesian traditional concepts within our ontological belief systems to explain the contemporary conflict of personality clashes and drama scenes of a woman in a diaspora environment trying to validate her status quo and identity.

It shifts through historical land marks and gains insights to incidental foot notes but is primarily a literary experimental novel about belonging. Just wanting to belong to a group identity as much as keeping up a personal space of validation in changing society.

The Papua New Guinea in which my grandparents lived in was a different place to the one my parents moved and traveled in their respective careers and raised me. Now the one I live in is more alien than they all care to remember it. This is as strange as this tale whose genre in their time would have been unheard of let alone been an object of socio political disgrace to our family's reputation.

The famous English Bard Shakespeare said that the whole world is a stage and we are all actors on the stage. Here

in the Pacific Islands, we are what we are: performers on a stage. Thus, we add further to this adage by acknowledged Knowledge of knowing that, "time is immortalised into a quiescent state until re-activated". But not so much a woman to speak outside of her engendered space about matters of the knowing. For they are part of the knowing in their keeping, "Kokoi fuyo!". The tone, the essence and guiding philosophical values attached to it.

Let me explain it here in this analogy. From my mother's story of something she had experienced some years ago.....

Just before Christmas this year when the government offices were starting to close their doors for the holidays, I was making my last errands for the year. Completing final tasks for my clients, rushing through the busy festive season traffic at Kimbe town. In the midst of honking cars, rushing crowd and the loud banter that emanated from within, with that scent of mixed odours, scents and town pollution was a sight that held my attention. The gentle steady sweeping of a street sweeper in front of Papindo shopping mart.

It was a bright cloudy day with a steady breeze unaffected by the human and automobile traffic nor the tide of noises all around. It was a passing fleeting image of a person doing his job gracefully to earn a descent honest wage in a growing urban town in one of the busiest times of the year.

He was using a coconut frond broom and with each sweeping motion he gathered the rubbish into a neat pile of fallen leaves, wrappers, discarded carton boxes and packages which he removed swiftly away from the public space. It was his action that made me stop and take notice of a memory buried long ago at a time when I first traveled out of the country on duty travel some years ago.

A different time, place, circumstances and country. Somewhere so far away in time frozen in the recess of my memory. The nostalgic aroma of brewing hot cappuccino, focaccia grilled cheese sandwiches and the busy traffic of a foreign country haunts me. I feel the numbness of dull ache of loneliness and trying to fit in whilst rushing to work on a cold wintery morning. The busy intersection of the traffic lights where a crowd of white people are moving and jostling past you as the traffic lights with the walk sign in green colours are flashing overhead.

A moment too brief in flashing scenes with emotional pull had momentarily gripped me causing me to pause and gaze. Like a pulse in a time sequence, I was drawn to that episodic interval of personal experience. It was as if time had stood still in a black and white phase of temporal warp. A lapse in the continuum of my awareness of reality that transcended between the now reality time frame and an event in my past in my memory. The trigger was the scene of the street sweeper, earnestly sweeping the busy road in Kimbe town.

That event in my life had been stored away in a state of quiescent existence until a similar activity in my present reality retrieved that memory of living through a similar atmosphere years ago but at a different place and time. This act of pausing acknowledgement in remembering, recollecting and restructuring my worldview reinforces the personal identity value-structures of me as an individual and indigenous person in my changing landscape. It is an act of awakening of my intellectual consciousness to the realities of time, spaces and different sequences that exists.

As for me it brings back memories of me and my parents together on a hill top of the summit in our plantation estate. A large family commercial estate of coconuts and cocoa. A scene that flashes through my mind with a bitter taste of the happier times. Reminisce

"Eerie! My island home, " my excited shriek could not be contained anymore in that moment. They came gushing out in a tumble. Streaming down my face in a warm rush and stingy with a bitter taste. It's sharp memories raw and tender pushing forth that dull aching feeling of missing. The sheer*

emptiness of longing for something so dear and precious as my childhood homestead starts to beckon me. Calling me, silently, home. To where my folks are. Papa and Mama and all my dear ones back on the main island of New Guinea.

I remember Mama's face as she summons me in her heart. Her words echoing in my mind.

"Dubo my child if you were here now instead of being away at university you would see this panoramic view. I remember the first time your papa Lolote showed you our piece of land."

"Where papa? you cried excitedly. The braided locks bobbed up and down on your head while you were looking eagerly over the valley below following the direction your father was pointing. You were only a small child then, five years old. Everyone who knows us say you are a miniature image of me your mother. This image of you with your excited and bewildered realisation of your heritage was private, sacred and belonged to three of us. Now I stand here alone years later recalling that moment.

There, over the horizon on mountain ranges in the distance the monsoonal rains are coming. Black clouds hover high above as darkness descends in gentle layered hues like doom gloom blooming looming echoes resonating in the distant winds. Tree leaves on scrawny branches rustle, rushing past in a breeze never stopping. Whilst, below in the forest floors nothing stirs.

Flashing splinters race across the open sky as tricklets and droplets fall like curtains that rise and fall in crescendos. It is as if nature and splendour appear for applause, with their roaring pride in spreading their monsoonal showers, sobbing in deep grieving feats. At the outset, I am reminded again that I wanted this and it is I that tries to see but cannot at all times agree for all our lives because the wet weather was as damp as the emotions ebbing from within.

Home was a distance across those silver linings that met the ocean blue lines over the sea a sinking longing that haunts the viewer looking out especially when you are far from home.

For many years now I seem to think that during the evening walk by the beach you start to understand the silent conversation going on there at the beach. It was as if the waves of the sea call out to bystanders. It is when you look more closely, it starts to sing in that silent tune of emotions. Playing magic in your wake, bringing to its brim the pressing sense for familiarity. Others would argue that nature in its intuitive way reads from your deepest desires of your wanting news of dear ones far away in homes across the ocean.

The final light fades away to the looming dusk with that majestic grace of the final bow.

Splashing waves bid farewell with surging tides and another day ends. In the passage of the fading light where the moon starts to make her grand entrance a seagull flies above the sea in a hasty retreat. Swirling and calling out to the day's keepers that the end of another day is now accomplished. It has ended in dark murmurs of the nocturnal gaze. Then deep sighs breathe in unison of grace ever so close so morose the bidding tale of the day's end.

It is the wettest month of the year now. The cold draughts at night sting our bones and rattle our teeth as we cling onto the threadbare bedsheets. During the daylight it is muddy and soggy outside. Debris is swept by the tide through over flowing drains onto road sides and foot paths while pedestrians run past them with hurried strides. There's something about the way people cope with the weather in order to meet their dead lines or complete tasks.

I received her email in the morning.

"Oh, Dubo how I miss you now as time stretches wide and reaches its long arms into the abys as I await your return to the village" she says, and relates the full tale…..

"The lap top battery has to be charged for us to speak on a video call but I don't like these gadgets. For one thing they use up the solar batteries and I need them for light. I have to ration as we agreed to do the monthly chat session to save power so I shouldn't be complaining but is it really for me or for you we having this session."

"Frankly, I don't care but it does get lonely on the island having only your dad to talk to. For a quiet person he is really struggling to accommodate my needs in having these conversations and it is putting a strain on us as much as it is becoming a constant feature of our married life now. The retired couple with grown up adult kids. That is how cruel life can become in the receding years, I think, and it has been only a few days since you left."

Chapter 12

Family Matters

Mama has been so exhausted these days by all these emotional attacks. So I am emailing you our family updates with her concerns. She says right now she is feeling so overwhelmed. "Are we not the better fools. I mean look at your sister Kaiymei?" She asks. "Your Sister Kaiymei" she emphasises again.

Every waking moment of Kaiymei's life Mama says, that she has lived, is a reminder of the good things in life. When the song "The goodness of life" is sung "I see Kaiymei's life epitomises the journey of intellectual holiness. We as a family are blessed to have her in our midst teaching us that life is a gift and privilege not to be taken for granted. That is why sometimes I get angry with your brother Dido when he doesn't realise how privileged he is in his life to be born with an able body."

Kaiymei is patient until when she feels defenseless against being attacked or forced against her will. These are the rare moment where Kaiymei airs her frustrations over her disability. These cries of frustrations are very difficult to console easily. She needs our prayers for this helpless frustration to become steps to triumph in her life.

Kaiymei's favourite hymnals these days are the traditional English hymns such as Amazing Grace, Nearer My God To Thee and Just A Closer Walk To Thee. In Amazing Grace, Kaiymei sings this hymn in the quiet hours of the morning when all seems desolate, bringing a reflective gaze into our lives and giving us hope. Whilst the hymn "Nearer My God to Thee" she will sing in a high beautiful melody of how we can move closer to God in every adversity we encounter in life. I had a paranormal experience recently where I dreamt of a new kids hymn from the African American folklore known as "Do Lord Do Remember Me?". This is a song she now hums in her quiet moments. Nonetheless, our prayers as parents have always been these:

For all the years and all the tears. As the fears wear away and we stare at all that we have come through. Sufferings that Kaiymei has endured locked inside them tears. Cries that we hear words that don't disappear. Oh Jesus, wipe away our daughter's curse and bring her back to us. You have laden her to her bed with a weight in her very being. Listening to all the kids playing outside is torment enough, don't her tears ever move the God whom she praises all of her life? We surrender her to your warm embrace. We pledge the holy blood of Jesus in her life; and commit her to your healing grace so she can live her life to the fullest. It is all we ask for our dear daughter.

Like the villain and the heroine with dual lenses we strive to pass the challenges, troubles and trials along the way. When we are forced to reflect in the resurrection of Jesus Christ on Easter we always come back to the question of "*What does Easter mean to you?*" We ponder upon the resurrection story and try to make sense of the great miracle that took place. There are countless times in our lives as Christians when we look at how our child suffers and we cannot comprehend and make sense of how a child so young can face such grave hardship in her short life yet still believing in God whole heartedly. It all becomes like a farce at the end of the day. There was no beginning nor any end. That is until Foroga*. It was a beautiful space.

Then there is you and your brother Dido. Did you know that I often see the parallel differences in your lives (Dido and yourself) in how you try to wade into the person you aspire to be.

Dido, is a restless philosopher who wanders around his social landscape trying to locate Utopia on earth. More specifically, in locating where the liberal state of personal liability rests upon himself because he wants to live his own life without being answerable to anyone. Whilst, at other times he seems to be someone that strives to be obscure from the limelight yet it is when in crowded circumstances he is drawn into situations where he must play his leadership role in society.

In a similar context, you too seem to display that trait of inferior complex in public spaces of engagement shying away from the limelight and responsibility of leadership unless it is forced upon to you.

Both your character traits have been a concern to us lately. To an extent where papa and I have been wondering out loud how you both do not have the confidence of stepping out of your comfort zones.

Then sometimes I am amazed how 'resilience' has been a part of our lives.

Now I started to realise that Dido takes it upon himself to go to the block with some of his friends and collects firewood or goes fishing and comes back to the house to contribute to the kitchen when we are down. "He has his own schedule and way of taking initiative in getting things done. There are times too that he sacrifices his health to go fishing until dusk so we can have protein in our meals as well. We had warned him that his body is still not able to cope with the cold at night. 'To avoid fishing at night, but he is like a stubborn horse as always. His bones on the chest are protruding through his skin and therefore dad wants him to go for tuberculosis tests."

It is now Sunday evening and dusk has enveloped the earth and the ends of the soil are emitting the coldness within them into the darkness all around as Papa and I await his return. Papa is in a grumpy complaining mood because he told Dido to go collect his fishing bait for the night fishing session he planned. Now he is fuming because he has not returned back home.

Dido did not come home that night (Friday). He returned in the evening the next day (Saturday) with firewood and bought Kaiymei's noodles. On Sunday morning he is doing his assignments in Social Science and English and Papa as usual is assisting him with their dramatic interactions. They read and try to make sense of the English words, terms and phrases. At one stage they both sat back baffled by the word "rim". After I defined it they continued on.

There are so many people who challenge Dido and try to put him into their own box of expectations but he has continued to maintain his assessment marks despite these setbacks. I had him change classes to Maka's class earlier in the year but Maka has been sick for long periods and that has affected Dido's punctuality. We have paid his school fees and have been consistent in the project fees including attending PNC meetings and commitments set for parents. We also replenished his school supplies so he can have more interests in school attendance. We are trying to make more effort with him in his school work and regularly monitor his attendance.

We also got him registered for confirmation classes at Ruango but he has failed to attend the classes and had his name scrapped off the list of candidates much to his disappointment. Papa as usual is teasing him and saying that it would be such a big embarrassment as an adult later in life to join younger candidates to get confirmation. In his typical way of saying *"better now or never"*.

I pen off here in the Afterword's of uneasiness about these pressing issues.

There are nights that I have spent tossing and turning unable to relax troubled by these unresolved issues involving and concerning my citizen's rights. These never-ending thoughts are pressing concerns that are unresolved, and need much deeper intense contemplation of what is, and needs to be done, to address the situation, circumstance and stature of events and individuals.

It is as if I need to raise these banners on the highest pedestal at the election site at election times.

There is too much petty talking trying to earn brownie points and at times tempers flare but money floats, cargo cults rise. But this is all cheap talking, wannabe doll manifestations become a farce and walk amongst us to belittle and erode the essence of the validity and relevance of the stature of our citizens rights. We look beyond the facade of glamour attached to this label for our fundamental membership in our sovereignty. After all, when glitter fades, people within our circles of influence create emotional and psychological little warfare.

On many occasions there have been bitter lies within those wasted eyes of his. Remember him? They were his giveaway feature of his very nature of honesty. Thus, giving away the misery he harboured in his life where his legal wife was on a constant war path with his numerous readily available lovers, and the second third fourth and whole 'wife' portfolio. Every one of them were up in arms with verbal assaults as fitting wives with sitting rights to his life, but it was his heart that no one consulted.

Nonetheless, the wet season had come with showers of money rains, cargo cult, flush funds of the land group with their free handouts in the village like streets of gold in his pocket, funds for bribes and corrupt deals but to these greedy women it was the colour of money that mattered more than the conscience or ethical just and honest sweat of compensation.

All these incidents are becoming obvious like the current rush in wind where there are no secrets under the sun. Where prayers spun turn a ton of God's good grace back on humanity. It is like what the old people would say, who used to caution us in our story telling around the warm fires at nights.

There was a woman walking away from me. From a distance I could see that she was clad in her traditional wear. She was weak, yet the bark straps on the grass skirt fluttered with each stride she took. Her arm bands were strewn with heavily scented herbs and while she carried a heavily laden bilum on her head. In one hand she held a rope that was tied to a piglet. I tried calling out to her there and then.

"He! Meri Wantok."

Was it me? A subservient breed? Just because I am plain and down trodden, not too loud, just broken I have become. She told me to carry a Bilum but she didn't want to see what was inside. She said it would ruin her sensibilities.

My bua *and kito* was cast aside while I modelled for the role of those placid renditions of an image that down-played a Meri Papua Niugini; that idealised the very image of us Ol meri wantok.

We become again another distorted notion of the media hype imagery while our voices are drowned by folly I wait for the next voyage and I am just about to board now to see whether reality is ever truly told. This is because I know that deep sentiments are seeping up in time and they will soon blow up. It is what stirs ethnic violence to brew while we sit in that segregated hateful and deteriorating relations, as late as we wait to pay the price. So all we ever ask for is to stop the blood of our sons from spilling on their ancestral lands.

Chapter 13

Night Raids

Then there was an incident last week that involved people at Kawutu; Dano and Walo. Its aftermath triggered the violent mob that optimistically rushed into our neighbourhood. They came into our place trying to make it seem our boys were involved. The two brother's in-law had a row that resulted in a bystander getting injured. However, an opportunist mob started to build at Kawutu and they descended into our hamlet thrashing and rampaging through our yards. Randomly raiding houses at will as they continued on with a rowdy banter creating confusion and tensions in the dark.

A big group ran on to the main road to search for Dano. Whilst an opportunistic mob led by Rambo went into Tangana Pogi brandishing their weapons. Upon hearing the commotion all the Sisi meris came out of their houses. They stood in front of their own yards looking in the direction of the noise. It was when Pupu Mara held up a torch directing straight into Rambo's face that she confronted him.

"Hey, what's going on? ", she asked bewildered at his intrusion in the night.

"Passim maus blo yu," (shut up), he yelled back at her waving his sharp bush knife in front of her.

"Aiyee! Mipla mekim wanem long yu na yu mekim displa pasin long mipla? "(What, why and how do you explain being in our yard tonight?) she yelled back at him.

Pointing the edge of the knife at her face he continued to yell,

"Klia, em wei? Em wei? (Move away, where is he? Where is he?)

"Yupla haitim em wei?," (where are you people hiding him?) he growled loudly in a belligerent tone.

"Aiyee, yu toktok long husait?," (who do you think you are?) the old women all screamed back in a unison.

"Dano!"

*"Mipla painim Dano!" (*We are looking for Dano*).*

*"Noken giaman, em wei?" (*Do not tell lies to us, where is he?*)*

*"Yupla maski long haitim em." (*Do not hide him.*)*

"Salim em kam arasait," he yelled back at them.("Bring him out to us.")

"Oi! Yu mas long long, man ya haus blo em arasait?", the old women cried out in unison. (You must be insane to even ask such a question For goodness sake the person you are looking for is your own neighbour.")

"Yu painim wanem na kam insait olgeta long hap blo mipla. Mipla ino birua blo yu" they all cried back at him again. (What are you trying to prove here coming into our yard at this time of the night?).

"Yu ok oh? ", Pupu Mara shouted back at him." (Are you in the right sense of mind or not?)

"Yu kam rough long mipla long wanem?" Next week Wok Kastom blo yu yah bai husait gen bai helvim yu?," She angrily spat on his face. (How dare you come in this manner; next week who will come and help witness your ceremonial festivities and rites of passages ceremonies?)

Rambo stood still as if in a daze unprepared for the old woman's bold aggressive confrontation. He started to lower his knife when he instinctively bent down and a knife slash missed his head.

He slipped onto the ground before standing up in a daze and dashed off. The boys at Pogi haus boi sprang into action picking up weapons and ran after them. The mob that followed Rambo scattered in all directions. One of the groups ran along the track to Papa Lincoln's house. They stoned aunt's house as they broke into Papa Lincoln's tenants house robbing them off their credit card, mobile phone and other furniture bore trashing all their eating utensils and taking off.

Those that went to the main road eventually regrouped and met at the Ruango catholic mission junction, stoning Pupu Croka' s house. For a few minutes the whole yard was lit with fire crackers dispersing them. There was shouting, shoving, people running everywhere. It was like fire crackers exploding on New Year's Eve celebrations. However, the crowd eventually dispersed.

Silence descended back on the streets, people went back into their houses and closed their doors. The show was over but the fear was real and remained. A cool breeze filtered through the windows with the curtains stirring and twisting as dawn was approaching like an errand boy, with lithe movements, as everyone slept. They slept lightly cautious and alert for any sound of noise.

During the commotion Papa was at Pupu No'oh's house. He had seen everything and had not realised who was involved. While I had been standing at our water pump when Watermelon called over and told me to check Dido. There were young boys running around in the melee. No, I replied he is with his dad and they are both outside at the nambis ples visiting Dido's grandfather. However, after a few minutes had passed and the commotion had subsided Papa came home. Seeing him striding in with no care in the world I got him to look for Dido because of what Watermelon had just said. With an angry sigh, mumbling to himself, Papa went to New camp.

I had been doing the dishes a bit of laundry and bathing. Now refreshed I sat waiting for their return. Papa entered the house and Said that Dido was at the haus boi at his "amu's" place. With a deep sigh of relief I laid down to sleep next to Kaiymei. Whilst, Papa took a bath and had his dinner very late in the night.

The new day raised people in a quiet but restless way. Papa went to Tagana Pogi to follow up on what happened and met Dano. Dano told him that at dawn he went to Rambo's house and asked what he wanted from him. He told him, he was here now at his house and he wanted to know why he (Rambo) had organised a mob to hunt him around the whole village. He said that Rambo was speechless and unable to answer as were the other men who had joined in the hunting spree.

We would later be told that Dano was in the second group to enter nambis ples and confront the rampage mob. At the first crack of dawn Pupu No'oh had mobilised the boys and they descended on the men at nambis ples belting them telling them to teach their sons how to respect. Moreover, they were to pay compensation for the havoc they created last night.

At day break soon after Dano's men had left nambis ples they were unaware that Pupu Lo'oh and aunty Melva arrived a few minutes after their departure. They descended on the nambis ples men berating their behaviour for the previous night's incident demanding them to pay for the damages they had caused. Witnesses said the guilty culprits were reduced to mere laughing stock. Speechless, they were unable to explain their actions.

Papa sat with the boys as they compiled their statements to be submitted to the police station. He assisted Pupu Rick, Pupu Crocka and Pupu No'oh to resolve it. Dano's dad came into Pogi and contributions of *"bel kol moni"* were counted and brought out to people's nambis to restore peace with the injured party's family.

They were waiting for Pupu No'oh to arrive but when the time dragged on Papu Croker told Pupu Rick and Dano's father to go settle the peace arrangement and they would go about their business. Outside at the injured party's area they were surprised to see Papa become the go between peace negotiator. He had to convince them to receive the peace offerings so the tensions could cool on both sides of the warring parties.

Five pela ten pram tambu shell money, or a hundred- and thirty-Kina cash, was given over by Dano and his family to Walo. Sisi man held both Dano and Walo hands to signify peace as pram tambu was handed over with the money. Family members of the two warring sides stood in the distance watching the session take place. People who had bought land from the warring sides had also taken up arms to support their landlords. Tension filled the air as Papa walked from either side of the injured person's family for them to accept the peace offering. Now his body was aching as his stomach grumbled.

Although, the guilty party had given something to the injured party they did not even offer a glass of water or give betelnut to the village elders. It later unravelled that the injured person had never been initiated to the local community by his parents. By virtue of Kastom Wok the uncle of the boy should be in the peace negotiations but as the mother did not know how to perform Wok Kastom ceremonies for her children she did not know who to approach to represent her child.

Nor to follow cultural protocols in this situation. She did not reprobate the gesture and did not even acknowledge the peace negotiators on that day. The peace ceremony concluded around three o'clock and Papa came back to the house exhausted. It had been an eventful day. It was his first time to step in and resolve a difficult situation where one of his nephews was injured. However, it was more disgusting to witness and experience one of his sister's lack of awareness of cultural etiquette and protocols in society.

Wish you were here to witness how Tamana and Kina Gelu behaved throughout the Dano incident.

Tamana Gelu as usual, like Lucifer the snake, waited until all the peace negotiations were over before visiting the victim at night demanding that, as an uncle to the victim, he wanted pram tambu. He was given some and went home. A day later we found out by accident because the victim's mother wanted to return the pram tambu that stopped the *"ai blo spia."*

He was watching in the background as if nobody noticed. He went outside to the instigators of the incident conversing and transpiring with them as we slept at night. However, his own actions were noted and he was being watched by people who had been suspicious of his actions.

The next morning, we found out about his deceit when the mother of the victim had come looking for Papa. She had not even acknowledged Papa's role in the peace negotiation nor appreciated the intervention of the village elders who had stepped in to settle the aggrieved situation. Now she came shamelessly demanding to see Papa.

Upon seeing Tamana Gelu, she told him that she wanted the pram tambu she had given to him to be returned so she could go return them to the village elders. That's how we heard she had dispensed of the pram tambus. Papa was shocked and infuriated that she could even suggest returning the peace gifts. He chided her and sent her off.

She said that she was not satisfied with what was given and wanted a bigger settlement agreement. However, she did not know the traditional cultural protocols to demand such compensation payments. Here was Papa's elder sister, and she was unfamiliar with traditional cultural protocols. Here too was Tamana Gelu interfering into the peace settlement by purchasing peace gifts when they were just traded. How naive can these people be?

Apparently to them traditional shell money was just a token in which it was given from one Wok Kastom but had no significant role in practical living. Yet when everyone in our hamlet was contributing to the peace offering basket, Tamana and Kina Gelu were nowhere to be seen.

Tension was rife and the youths were carefully scrutinising their movements. They had seen them sneaking to nambis ples at the climax of the melee so their loyalty was being questioned. Kina Gelu was unusually quiet, mumbling to herself because they knew we were monitoring the situation. It is as if they are sitting on borrowed time in borrowed space.

Part 3

The Gelus [Micro Politics of Belonging]

Eresaka, (And You Are Doing it, So you Say)

Chapter 14

Introducing Tamana and Kina Gelu

Dear Caitlin, here are a full set of Mama's dairies on the Gelus for your reading. It is not easy reading. I must warn you. There was that issue of sanity when it comes to living next door to Kina Gelu and her husband here in our village. I like to think that we are another typical ordinary village in the south Pacific with our own issues and challenges. As Melanesians we have our way of resolving disputes, tensions and grudges and getting on in life. We have a good system of respect and values that guide our actions. That is until money and Christianity brought its own ideas and divided us all with this mixture using indoctrination of ideas that divided us by the colour of money and Creed ...

Oh Dubo!

How can I put into words the outright blatant acts and behaviour that has transpired from them lately? All the sneering and jealous strife ridden scenarios our family has encountered from them. I am telling you now my child that Tamana and Kina Gelu are being the most popular of sour grapes here, eternally trying to act like sophisticated idiots with empty drums appearing in an imaginary Filipino drama with a tantrum of tantrums. There are so many incidents far and wide and in-between, I will have to tell you the most harrowing here.

They were on the financial ride treating us with disdain and mocking us constantly using money as emotional blackmail or rather like an instrument of torture. Mind you this is not from the kind of money that is straight. You know what I mean?

Not money from the sweat of their brows but money taken as loans to finance their life style. Money that came as a school subsidy for financing the local elementary school infrastructure project such as classrooms and school fences, that is distributed by the management board including Mr Gelu. So, since his election this misuse of school funds has been a support to the unneighbourly tyrant over all of us.

Kina Gelu has got this attitude that money overrides our village social rules of etiquette and protocols for in-laws that is practiced here in the village. She thinks she is above all these traditional rules because of the colour of money she holds. This year when the school year started, she dressed like a plastic doll, grooming herself with makeup to walk around the village hamlets. Most people hid in their houses when they saw her coming down their street. Grown men and women, fathers and mothers of children, were scrambling into their bedrooms to hide behind curtained windows to watch her passing parade of lunacy. They were all laughing and pointing out jokes on her as she passed, taking their children by surprise. All of whom watched with curious faces of bewildering stares.

It took the street market ladies time to react but when they realised what was happening, they turned around and away from Kina Gelu's passing by pretending to count their loose coins on the table. They lifted their brows as she went by trying to hide the rushing giggles bursting through. Yet Kina Gelu thinking so highly of herself paid no attention to the public reaction. All that she wants to make known is that she can be a professional working woman in the village. So she wears high heels on the sands, flashing her painted lips as she smiles like a super model on a glamour shoot, only there are no cameras nor any crew. There are only the sneers and laughter of small children imitating her strange ways.

As each passing week went by we noticed how early in the morning she was making it habitual to yell at the top of her voice so the whole neighbourhood could hear that her children are wearing school shoes and carrying school bags. This is because not many people in the village can afford school shoes for their children and in many instances only wear thongs. Similarly, most of them carry their school books in string bags their mothers and sisters weave. Kina Gelu's loud comments were a form of self-promotion.

Not that it bothered anyone because fashion trends did not matter in our village or amongst our village folks. For them, clothes had a functional purpose rather than making a social statement. The irony in this was that whilst everyone had different opinions on what type of bags to carry or footwear to wear, Kina Gelu made it seem like the cheap Asian made products at the local China shops were luxury items.

During that fashion parade down the street she gave out a general impression that it mattered to her how she dressed. For good fashionable clothes to her is the ultimate mirror of success for a local village. Like a measuring yardstick of wealth. So she works tirelessly spending money on those cheap brands that look trendy at the local second hand shops that sell reused rags from charities in Australia. Every other day before school starts she does the family laundry manually by hand at the local village creek like a maniac. Scrubbing and rinsing, shaping and bleaching those rags maniacally.

Just the other day Mama heard Watermelon complaining of Kina Gelu's behaviour. "For the life of me I do not know how this phase or craze has descended upon them lately", she scoffs as she throws a sneering glance to the Gelu's' house.

Mama recollected how the Gelu's funny behaviour had transpired to this extent. It had become apparent soon after you had left the village for university, that on several occasions she had this intense feeling of someone staring down on her.

Every time she turned around, she looked straight back at the Gelus' glares. Deep scorching and searing staring back with a daring confrontational hatred direct at her. The naked rawness of emotions at times shocking. More often than not, when Mama caught them off guard, they scrambled to get out their cell phones as if trying to call someone. On more than one occasion talking loudly on the phone so Mama could see that they had phones. Mama said that she ignored them of course and continued whatever she was doing at that time.

Most days after school the Gelus encourage their children to watch movies on their cell phones on full blast so people passing by can see what their children are up to. More like a rhythmic slur vibrating truthful Chants out loud. When we are trying to cook or read in the afternoon there is that loud blast of movies on cell phones so distracting and annoying it makes you wonder out aloud "who let the deaf people out of the asylum?".

During these bouts of attention seeking feats both husband and wife drank at night, walking around aimlessly in public places in the village displaying their drunken dishevelled selves. The fact that they are both teachers in government public schools has no particular significance to them. To them the drunkard 'look' makes them feel young and trendy drinking till they come home bone dry. Often with spitting raging insanities, thrown at each other till they dropped into long slumbers at dawn. Despite trying to put on a good face early in the morning they could not take the responsibility to feed their children.

They are either too intoxicated or still drinking so could not cook breakfast for them. These are children all of whom are below the ages of twelve. Is this not maltreatment of children?

While their parents got drunk and boasted their financial affairs for the world to hear, their children were washing the pots and pans to prepare their meals. Sometimes there was no matches in the house to make a fire and they would go from kitchen to kitchen searching for a fire to cook a meal.

Every boast and public show was yelled out in a loud banter like a scorn and sarcasm at life. Like the deranged mad woman screaming out to be heard in a polite society. It was as if the angry spoilt brat of a foolish woman had become loose, trying to justify their vanity in vain. Instead of the public envy they were seeking, it bore them the alienation of social inclusion in private homes of the elite circles no matter how hard they tried.

This irritating drama was like an itch that could never go away no matter how you scratched it. It left grazes on the skin stinging you with the itch. Now it's a double irritation on the skin that needs attention before it creates more damage so you become more intent on looking at what is causing it to itch. What is its source? What is causing the Gelus to annoy us unceasingly?

It is definitely not so good when your neighbour goes on to intentionally harm you with their good fortunes. In a village where you are blood relatives it is not our culture, not our way, but how do you transmit that message without causing a scene?

Mama continued, here they were trapped in this situation, of a flaunted lifestyle of material things, exhibited to us and our children as if Father Christmas had arrived earlier than usual. But was it real or just a show to be seen? It all looked a bit strained and more like a social cloak to hide away the imperfections of a family.

How you feel the weight of that sheer emotional stress in her description of incidents that persists week after week after week. Here she stresses that every week is disastrous and feels like you are being punched below the belt. As the proverbial words rang many times, so too our family's vulnerabilities worsened. Our financial situation was in dire straits literally using the slang *"eye blo dog white"* to describe our circumstances compared to the Gelus. During which they were obviously thriving, exhibiting their consumer goods to our eyes like a mockery. Their children were holding their phones and openly taunting Dido at every opportunity. So during one of those unbearable occasions Mama told our brother in a stern voice, loud for all to hear, warning him with them listening in from our kitchen,

"My son, I would rather give you the tools for you to make it in this world than material things which will be of no use to you in the future. Take a good look around you son, haven't you realised that all the children whose parents had given them mobile phones and boom box are now in the village. We gave your elder sister tools to survive; to listen, observe and have respect for elders' advice not material things like mobile phones and now she is trying to find her place in society. Either you become a show off now and use mobile phones like an empty drum in the village fashion trend cat walk, or work hard and learn the basics of surviving so you will be someone in the future. That is my principle as a parent".

From that day onwards, the mobile phone taunts, including loud movie sessions in the neighbourhood subsided. Included were Kina Gelu's phone call boasting sessions loudly broadcast in the midnight hours for all to hear. The nonsense, point scoring attitudes also dissipated for a while. It ebbed through like a season of *"wanna be"* charades they engineered to shame us.

Alas, like many evil antagonists and plots, that brief interlude from their psychological taunts only lasted a while before they started another round of psychological attacks. This time it involved the boundary flower window-dressing mime show.

Ha! Mama drew a huge sigh, saying "This guy would win an Oscar award for playing the role of one of Adolf Hitler's hench men for terrorising neighbours. Probably the Melanesian village ignorant tyrant." It became a comical farce for our family.

Watching Tamana Gelu watering flowers three times a day in our tropical humid climate is verging on erratic. The poor flowers could not stand such lethal doses crushing them from under the weight of the hot water flooding over them when he watered during the hot midday heat. The soil into which he planted the flowers was on a swampy patch that drained water. Every time it rained, he also diligently watered them without thinking or noticing how he was flooding them. We laughed so much till our bellies ached before I put an end to the drama by telling him to his face how foolish he looked in this charade. It was after that the planting effort were abandoned.

In the course of all these dramas unfolding, there was a stream of people arriving in our home. Everyone had their own issues to be resolved. As it was a diverse group, all of them raised wide ranging issues that needed my consultations. For a while they were deterred and yet they came back with another scheme to outwit us.

Chapter 15

The Plot Thickened

The fact that they can buy mobile phones to show off, that they can download and watch movies to disrupt my zoom conference sessions is intimidation, used to disrupt and irritate all our plans at every opportunity they can. The fact that I can do conferences all around the globe while they watch pornography all night on high volume distinguishes our values and outlook in life.

I am traveling on uncharted waters of my life and that of our peoples' destiny and these people with very narrow mind set and cannot see beyond their bedroom, think that the work I do is of no significance. Or at least, of very limited relevance to anything they have ever experienced in their lives. I am therefore reminded of my artworks criticism, of the government's ongoing colonialist plunder and land grabbing policy decisions affecting our people.

How can we blame this couple who are teachers by their own standards but remain as ignorant as the bulk of the literate out-of-school population in the country.

This is because they cannot comprehend government policy issues nor understand basic government functions and bureaucratic processes that administer the delivery of government service to our citizens.

During which Kina Gelu has the habit of unintentionally boasting her ignorance in the neighbourhood. Like she doesn't know that a bank loan is actually borrowing money and raves on to all who can hear their family's financial liabilities. The fact that she has found a new English word without knowing its definition is as hypocritical as life's drama can be in our neighbourhood.

Yet I am saddened by the fact that we have to put up with idiots like this, to create master pieces in art and life.

Tamana Gelu also tried another mind-technique to intimidate us after the flower garden fiasco. He went on a three-times-a-day regime of raking his small yard and deliberately overriding our boundary, making a huge show to come rake in from of our kitchen. Just as well it so happened that after the disaster of realising, we were laughing at his flower incident he stopped.

Here in our village, life continues as it usually does gentle and undeterred by all the circumstances, situations and politics taking place. Like a sleeping giant it embraces all who seek its embrace like the abode of the living dead. Your departure was like the opening of a new well in which we can see our reflection. A wishing well that reveals the secret thoughts of people we come across ON our paths in life. For instance, like those so-called Wannabes in our village. They like to flaunt their money carelessly in front of us making us feel like social outcasts in society in the most condescending cynical way.

Chief amongst them being the Gelus, of course, our nearest neighbours. We started to recognise their attitude issues as soon as you left. We noticed that on the very next day after your departure Tamana Gelu and his wife, Kina were going to great lengths to get our attention. A public attention-grabbing vendetta immersed in hatred to show their jealous streaks. Like the time when they both took great lengths of making loud noises, exclamations and announcements to show off their kids going to school. In our traditional culture, our Korafe people call these type of behaviour *sorara** to antagonise someone out of your own jealousy. So the phrase I would use as follows,"*ni isesa awa ne taka Soara uhseri*"which could be interpreted as "*the day you departed our shores, the jealousy within their hearts was spun to large proportions.*" It was as the day the wind spirit arrived in our lives. How they treated us when we were around them made us become self-conscious of ourselves when we are in their presence.

Despite changing our family's social narrative in the village economic landscape with your educational status, the reality we face is far removed from prosperity. We feel the pinch of our dire circumstances, trying to make ends meet so you can achieve your dreams and goals. Every day we live a hand to mouth existence. We had to scrape through the days so food could be put on the table. We all had to beg to survive. It was as if the scent of poverty stretched its long talons into our wealth, trying to drown us in debt.

How did we come to this stage is a question that has been haunting us ever since. Despite all the prayers and soul searching, we were left to drown in the tide that was surging before us. In this state of self-consciousness, we were more alert to our own circumstances compared to that of those around us. To a large extent this spiritual reconstruction of our family fortune was through a process of cleansing involving the redirecting our priorities as a family. That process towards prosperity is painful as it is.

Now that I have come to think about it, it was as if a supernatural presence had been unleashed over our lives. Through the Christian analogy it is as if evil came to sit on our roof eating up goodness and prosperity of our family. From the pit of her belly, she gnawed at our efforts. She taunted us mercilessly despite our pleas and through no fault of our own she tugged and pulled in all directions to destroy us.

What with the large rats, the toads, the Gelu's campaign, the scraping for food and joy, and in the face of our prayers, the evil remained.

Again, the willows howl relentlessly outside my windows. It's been raining these past few days as if it's any explanation of their keening. They are being tossed and rattled by the frenzy of the storm. The tree acted like there no end in sight of this natural calamity and wanton madness.

And again I must also mention that on our island the old people often remind us that everyone came into being by being born with the same song in our memory but each had their own tune and melody. Like the morning bird that praised the new day. Plants bloom in their greatness but it is us humans that have lost the ways of praising the richness of life and appreciating the fact that we are alive and blessed to live another day.

Indeed, the wet season this year had begun early and it has been raining for several days now nonstop. Just that endless heavy patter thrashing and crashing from the sky. Those intermittent pauses in between the growl, rumble and roar in quick successive bursts, streaks and flashing light. Sudden and illuminating in the dark. An invisible battle fought on our turf without us seeing the silhouettes stretched out in the shadows trying to claw away our skin with its chilling air. Meteorologists predicted this unusual phenomena, calling La' Nina.

This morning out on our family beach front there is an ugly sight of mounting debris that has come in on the night tide. Uprooted food crops from gardens submerged by the flooding. Murky brown thick water rushes at the banks of rivers into the open sea. The track to the beach is littered with muddy puddles. It is an uninviting scene people are avoiding unless it's absolutely necessary to use the track.

I heard on the morning breakfast news that Dagi bridge was submerged in the raging flood last night. The social media platforms have been going viral with the images of the storm damage happening here. Somehow the echoes of its raving madness continue to cloud out my subconscious state. I guess I am still overwhelmed by it all. The weather resonates with our emotional issues here.

It is like being into a dark spectre of the supernatural powers beyond our control. We were under spiritual attack in a battle field we were unprepared and ill equipped to handle. A battle of wills raged within us trying to put a thorn in our paths. We were like puppets on a stage being drawn into a play in whose script we could not rehearse but only improvise.

These shocking fresh insights into our lives are like a new awakening. The realisation that people we respected as friends wear masks before us and reveal their true voices when our circumstances change. In the midst of our troubles their rear heads appear when their expectations are not met. Issues you faced have become public broadcasts in liabilities.

Chapter 16

The Tyrant Mind Games

I had just brushed off that odd defensive cautious stance from walking past Back Page and Rambo and this incident, soon after those public snubs, further exacerbated my anxiety for the day. Yet the good thing was it increased my weariness when reading people's body language towards me. I have been passing them in Morekea town and feel that air of indifference coming from them. A predatory consciousness and silent look of mirth from Rambo and his family as much as Back Page and her family. They walk on in a hunched-up frame trying to shield their naked intent. Like a dog with a bone to pick, they shuffle their legs in front of them to shift the dust on the shoes of their feet.

Oh Dubo! Again……

All that sneering and jealous strife meted out on our family. I am telling you now my child that Tamana and Kina Gelu are the worst of these sour grapes trying daily to compete with us. Trying to act like sophisticated idiots with empty drum intelligence. It seems as if they are on a constant move, treating us with disdain and mocking us with their accessibility to acquire cash. More specifically, they look down on us as with disdain in their midst because they have the means and capacity to do so. In other words they use money as a consumer passion for the never ending need for materialistic acquisition.

To an extent their actions and general demeanour is such that money is the identity of wealth. An unruly, undisciplined mask to hurt others and those they consider below their level of social status. Actions that have become spiritual weapons of hate manifested into instruments of psychological attack against us.

Mind you this is not their money, as everyone now knows.

Every morning just as we are having breakfast accompanied by Kina Gelu's loud broadcasts of self-pride and preservation: her children's new attires including school shoes and bags. Still no thought from her that many people in the village cannot afford this. Everyone has a different opinion on what type of bags to carry or foot wear to wear but to Kina Gelu but she still parades the cheap Asian made products as luxury items. She knows no better.

One could assume that she sees dressing up to her is the ultimate mirror of success. The measuring yard of wealth so she acquires money to spend on those cheap brands that look trendy at the local second-hand shop. Then she does laundry like a maniac to maintain the articles durability and in subsequence, its spic and span sheen of fashion trend wear ability.

For the life of me I do not know how this faze of craze has descended upon them lately but I do know that it began soon after you had left our village. I remember that particular afternoon because of the intensity of the hate in their eyes boring down on me as I was doing laundry. I looked up from what I was doing to meet their stares in all it's undisguised hatred exposed and unguarded. As soon as I had looked, they both took out their cell phones talking loudly in the phone so I can see that they had phones. I ignored them of course and continued whatever I was doing much to their chagrin. The daily dose of psychological attacks included the after-school sessions of high volume movie watching. At nights husband and wife drink themselves bone dry.

These sessions end up in a brawl between themselves with a string of verbal assaults that lead to full assaults and screaming matches with each other. Then just after midnight they fall into deep long slumbers. By dawn they both are both early risers who take the responsibility to feed their children early before going to school. Every so often people who approach them are particularly hostile when their loud banter was disturbing the quiet night before. Often they are too drunk to get up and cook so their children do the dishes and cook breakfast as they listen to their music on the phone in a drunken stupor.

More often the parents spend all the money on getting drunk they forget to buy even a box of matches to make fire and cook breakfast.

Tamana Gelu also tried another intimidation activity soon after the flower garden planting and crazy watering fiasco. This routine involved three times a day regime of raking his small yard deliberately overriding our family's hedge rows. On this occasion of provocation, he made a huge show to come rake inside our yard walking distinctively and threatening in our yard right in front of our kitchen. We simply ignored him and pretended that he did not exist as we moved about clearing and cleaning our lawns and flower gardens.

Then there was the phone calling mimicry that both Tamana and Kina Gelu had orchestrated towards us trying to get our attention. When you left and you started calling us at night, Kina Gelu would get free credit calls from the retail distributor of the phone companies so that she could call her friends and relatives who lived a few blocks down the street at around midnight. When this session of mimicry was conducted was around about midnight and the village was quiet as deaf in silence so her voice could be heard in its piercing shrill pitch during these conversations. Driven by their conceited and condescending hatred she played this role with such sinister mechanical cold tones creating morbid scenes of contention in our neighbourhood. We just continued to ignore them making them angrier and huffing, groaning and mumbling as they walk past us.

They also used these phone sessions to turn their children into vessels through which they could channel their hatred towards us as a family. On this occasion they brought each of their children's mobile phones so they could each watch movies on their own devices.

These were expensive cell phones, luxury items that were treated as mere toys to spite people in our neighbourhood. This turned out to be a gross village folly, as our local people watched with disdain and not respect. For we could only see through the whole charade and chide them within their ear shot how foolishly they were, becoming the village clowns who had somehow discovered the devices of modern technology.

As for me, your Mama and yes, I repeat yours truly, took the extreme response where I somehow devised coping strategies to deflect their emotional and psychological attacks. This strategy was to throw back at them the sarcasm they meted out to us. So one time as Kina Gelu went through her routine of calling friends two blocks down the street with much entertainment of loud dialogue and monologue at our end it looked more like a boastful

swipe at us. It was done with much regal activity like a prom queen parade show live performance, so I too put up my own rendition with a counter banter performance. During which I pretended that I was having a phone conversation loud enough for them to hear within their hearing range: *"Yeah, exactly she is a lying bitch while her husband was away during the holidays she was drinking paia wara under the taro leaves at Kaibo and now since her husband's arrival she got him wrapped around her fingers."*

I saw Tamana Gelu sitting quietly under his house trying to hear more as his wife walked away disgusted. She mumbled and grumbled in protest walking up their veranda. On another such pretend phone conversation I said,

"Aiyo mipla isave lukim live Filipinos dramas long peles. Ol lain ol ino save lon lukim fon pes taim wans ol save blastim volume long movie na music so whole village can lukim longlong blo ol" in tok pisin". (Aiyo, nowadays we are privileged to watch live performance dramas in the neighbourhood in our village. We got people who just discovered the modern devices of mobile phones yet we think they are gadgets for watching movies and listening to music so we turn up the volume to full blast so our neighbours can see our very stupidity.)

Thereafter this whole mobile phone harassment sort of faded away. Even though, they were still using the devices but not so much with the grand display of entertainment and public show. However, within weeks their children's phones were either stolen or misplaced with their accompanying accessories. Now only the parents devices are used for these purposes. Yet as far as the contention for attention is concerned this has somehow been subdued over time.

What sweeping tides of time, phew!

Chapter 17

The Evil Psychopaths Games

Writing this for you, I have realised their very self in the drama that has transpired. For instance, when I look at the character traits of Kina Gelu, this is what I surmise her nature to be and how it has come to the point where she is behaving as reported here. All I can say is that since you left you have carved out the hole in her toxic bucket from which she has been leaking wastes on human virtues.

Although, she has a mobile phone she only knows the basic functions of a phone. Notwithstanding, she flaunts this ignorance in its entirety trying to look self-important. So watching movies has been her public past time. She thinks that the phone is for watching movies and calling friends only.

Anyway, we noticed how she has been using the phone at length, with unusual behaviour at times. It so happened that eventually, we found the cause of her unusual activity. On that particular occasion, the phone batteries had run out so she took it to charge at your sister Hegu's house. By the time the battery of the phone became fully charged the screen came on with a pornographic video playing. The kids screamed and mama Mae switched off the video on the phone. Soon the entire village heard of this incident.

In some way, it explains her behaviour of wearing mini thigh caressing shorts to the one-stop-market these days. Must be chemical fusion in her hormones from watching that stuff I guess. Even so, there have been consistent rumours about her unfaithful liaisons in the community, so she has constant issues of trust with her husband. To make it worse she often tells her husband in public *"I was not supposed to marry you"* provoking her husband to call her *"paia rais"* a derogative statement meaning "harlot" or "whore" in public. On more than one occasion they became violent in public where in fits of drunken jealousy they had a violent confrontation involving Tamana Gelu assaulting Kina Gelu. These domestic violence incidents mean they showcase their dirty linen in full public display with an audience listening. Like a reality show. It sort of made me think about how I had commented that their actions are like being in a Filipina drama reality show.

However, there are some in our community who have commented on their behaviour as the classic traits of a marriage built on the foundation of 'no shame'. In the village our people speak the indigenous Bebeli language and practice the traditional values and norms prescribed within its cosmological and ontological cultural frameworks. To a large extent our people practice intellectual humility as a socially accepted code of behaviour. So it is as if Kina Gelu actions are in direct opposition to this.

As a couple they are representative of the contemporary couples who live and behave outside of the precepts of the ethnography of shame. For the act of shame is part of the act of intellectual humility. For in the acts of shame are the actions of remorse and in turn self-respect being restored. This is not realised in these public dramas they instigate. So instead of intellectual humility Kina Gelu displays the actions of a naive and foolhardy woman wanting a status quo without knowing how to achieve it. Too many times she has shown through her actions that she thinks that they are attached to the materialism of a consumer driven culture. As a consequence, this has had them fit into the social crowd seeking couples without traditional lineage to their kin and all ancestors. A confused identity crisis in marriage and an unaligned family unit in the traditional framework of political foes and alliances. Thus, the general loss of respect in the community.

Sometimes she gets so intoxicated she walks around the nambis peles hamlet along the waterfront area of our village. She goes there with a boom box with the music on full blast and a group of young boys with whom she shares a plastic container of home brew. This is during her after work hours when she is not working as a teacher's aide. At day break she makes a grand entrance on her front yard with the music blaring on her shoulders. Never mind her flushed face and the tattered muddied state of her appearance, all she can feel now is the high sense of euphoria through her drunken state as the blaring music soothes and calms her nerves. On these occasions when she returns home, she orders her husband and children to bring her food without explanation or remorse over her actions.

One morning recently Tamana Gelu asked his wife for the first time where she had spent the night. It was a first time for this confrontation to take place after her night out.

Taken by surprise she replied that she had spent the night sipping home brew and listening to music on her boom box with a group of young boys near the big village river at nambis peles. That was as far as he could go with a confrontation. He chose to accept her explanations without any second thoughts. Thereafter, coffee and full breakfast awaited her prepared by him after her night out drinking with a group of young boys. It was during those drinking sprees that she had developed a great fondness of the freshly rolled tobacco in newspaper scrap wrappers called 'lus'.

She thinks it's chic to smoke these with the boys in 'group drags'. Taking long drags in the front yard she calls greetings to outsiders that pass their house, so they can see her in her drunken state. It is just one of the many long charades of role playing she adapted during your absence.

The first of which of course was in the beginning of the year where she had taken on the role of pretending to act like the office women in Kimbe town. She puts a loud entertainment show trying to get the public to notice her. **Oh yes, then there was that incident of the tyre Bilong Wheels.** When you were leaving remember those two girls that came over to stay with Tamana and Kina Gelu? Remember those pigs and the maintenance they did on their house? Well, it sort of reminds me of an adage that goes like this, *"everything that glitters is not gold"*.

It was as if the devil had all of a sudden possessed their souls. The powers of darkness started to descend into their hearts with mirth and jealousy reeking inside and out like oozing pus. So vile was their very presence in our midst it was like a vault of toxic evil. Their lives became the playing field for the devil. Twisting lies inside and out of them, about how they could hurt us.

Their hatred for our family was so intense Kina Gelu could not contain herself. They opened the Pandora box they had been keeping buried in their hearts as the principals of darkness gathered around them. We noticed the imps of greed, lust and pride roamed freely into their homes as they went into an overdrive trying to make their mark with all their material possessions to impress everyone. They were shoved around by the imps to carry themselves as self-important, but we all built walls of ignorance. Their whole idea of success is to contend opinion and subjugate others; it is one of suppressing others into an oppressive circumstance. Whilst ours is to seek God's countenance on our lives and the pathways He chooses for our lives. That is the difference between their ideals and ours in how we manage our family affairs.

At first it was to do with opening their private space at home to student boarders from the local junior high school. They wanted to emulate our own experience in hosting Moana and Hegu recently. This naked ambitious venture became more apparent when she was calling people in the near midnight over the phone to boast of her husband and their good fortunes in life. Much to everyone's chagrin the girls left their home for various reasons before term one ended.

Maltreatment allegations by Kina Gelu were cited, due to her treating them as mere free labour in the house. Lola's mum, your aunty Teresa, eventually had a row with them and then placed Lola with Watermelon and family. Whilst, the other, Bali girl's parents had given the four piglets as down-payment for her upkeep with them. By the time the Bali girl wanted to leave the family, Kina Gelu accused her of stealing her clothes and personal items in the house. There was a court hearing over maltreatment allegations so Kina Gelu accused the girl of theft and asked Lola to be her witness.

Watermelon and her husband were incensed over Kina Gelu's attitude and intentions to use Lola without realising and acknowledging, or even apologising, for how they had treated her. So Lola continues to avoid Kina Gelu. As for the young Bali girl , she was eventually removed from the Gelus' and placed with her relatives at the village settlement near our village so she could attend school here at our junior high school.

On the other hand, the four piglets they were ogling over and showing off about, two of them were stolen and the other two remained. Eventually, they had to make appropriate payments for the young Bali girl's removal from their home to compensate for the piglets. As for their building the new house, in the structure, much of the fly wire and ceiling fixtures of the house had deteriorated and hung in disarray.

Kina wanted to move the hedge rows of flowers into our side of the yard, extending it into where our kitchen area was located. So, Papa showed Tamana the rambutan fruit tree you planted when we first arrived in the village all those years ago. Papa wanted to clarify the fact that he had already allotted where you kids would build your houses on the yard. The very fact that Papa had already mapped out your areas had been an eye opener for them.

Huh! You know how your Papa loves to spin a tale of reportage; he commented on how Tamana's face had grown wide with astonishment. He described how Tamana Gelu had taken huge gulps of fresh air before retreating to Kina Gelu with the new revelations. Nothing happened immediately but after two days of quiet contemplation, what ensued was they argued back and forth. On the third day they were able to resume their daily regime of triple times rake and sweep yard duties.

The sheer weight of contention had been ignited like fire now more than ever, as they became aware of our news and the future implications and weight of future decisions of inheritance were drawn.

My daughter, you could never guess how it felt just living next to them as my pocket broke into threadbare rags as they lived in luxury next door to me. It used to hurt more when I was reduced to selling vegetables at the local fresh food market. It was worse when the unbearable; humid weather stung my skin and there were no buyers to buy my produce. For every season and every weather I braved them all to put food on the table, clothe ourselves and send you pocket money. Until that day a stranger met me at the market and prayed over me.

He was a very ordinarily dressed person without any distinct nor unusual features about to indicate this spiritual encounter. It was just another encounter at the grocery market with me trying to sell some fresh veggies and he bought some with a gentle smile. A very radiant and carefree interaction that made me look at him intently. It was then that he gave me a knowing gesture of raising an eye brow at me.

"Susa", he said to me "I understand there is an incredible heavy pressures on your life right now", he gently remarked. It was then that he told me that he had a distinct intuition that I needed a prayer of healing, and he prayed over me. He had told me that I was under a deep spell and the person who put the spell on me, but he believes that this spell was now lifted. He also commented that soon those who were persecuting my family would be removed from our presence.

It sounded fanciful and I was a bit sceptical so I forgot about it until now. After all, we are practicing Roman Catholics so we become reluctant in engaging in local superstitions.

I remember the moment after that praying encounter as I was waiting to go home. A certain calmness swept over me as I saw five white egrets flying up above me. It had never happened before, not at this place in the middle of the town market.

Somehow they added some sense of familiarity to the scenery. It's placid dryness that seemed to sting beneath one's soul in a deep scorching ache that never goes away. It brought up memories. All long buried in time but slowly beginning to unravel in the sweeping tide. Pressing, piercing and sometimes frightening me with such intensity of emotions.

Because there and then I had not really come to understand the depth of my own sorrows, yearning, regrets untold sacred surging feelings. But there and then at that busy market stand on the roadside towards Kimbe I felt liberated from within. With light steps I strode home never really knowing what happened to me.

There and then, from that day, gradually but surely, I had noticed a change that came over me in my home and those within my circle of influence. The biggest change I saw was that Tamana Gelu had lost his temper and was in a fit of madness in temperament. He took his anger out on his family chasing them away from their home and hurling objects at them. He ransacked the house he had painstakingly built in a fury in one day. From then on there was constant rows and violence until the end of the year.

Also, I stopped going to the market as people hired me to handle their financial administrative work. I set up a consulting company and our lives started to improve thereafter. At the end of the year, when school was ending, Tamana Gelu was arrested for misappropriation of school subsidy funds. It ended this long-standing saga of personal competition with us. God knows how much I thank him for this.

Kina Gelu had to give up their family estates to pay Tamana Gelu's creditors and it was their ruin. They left for Kina Gelu's Island village on a remote atoll in the Pacific that was the last we heard of them till now.

Chapter 18

After notes from Mila about Mama's notes:

After weeks of rain the skies finally cleared up again. From my window I can see the sun rise from behind Mount Hobohobo. Just after, the morning birds end their chorus. The sun's warmth cascades all over the flower beds. Here there are neat rows of new blooms of fresh roses. The insects' buzz is insistent as dogs howl excitedly at them. Somewhere a rooster crows but it's the pigs whose grunts are the loudest. In the kitchen the smoke of the breakfast fire flitters through the bamboo thatched thin walls. Outside it forms wisps of mists in the dampness all around. Indeed morning has broken here on our island somewhere in the Pacific Islands. All the school children have since left for school it is just the adults going about their business. So it's all quiet. As the hours stretched an impregnated stillness descends over the village. A deep anxiety hovered in passing with a kind of restless silence.

She had not slept well that night. A bad dream had woken her last night. It was so deep and piercing she became terrified by its intensity. She had been afraid to resume her sleep troubled by that nightmare. A lamentation of the death echoed through her mind frightening her. It was nights like this that she missed her children. But now they had their own families to care for. Surely, would it not be wrong to ask a question to nature and God. Didn't mothers matter anymore? Can children never see the impact of their absence on their mothers? Then again she says, I will never know.

Then again it was much better now than before, when those village Antagonists used to live with them in the village. Then again it was not something you would confess to anyone.

They wouldn't know the difference between a mother's longing and loneliness as she was left there among her diaries that maybe one day she would be able to read it.

Like the fairy tales we often hear at bed times as children as we were growing up. This is one of my favourite versions. Of how evil, something sinister, an evil eye, is putting a living curse on someone. This story is an extract from an email conversation of a mother to her daughter telling her about the watcher. A time when evil was let loose on us that day you departed.

The evil sat perched on our roof top redirecting our wealth and fortune furiously as we embarked on trying to change our family narrative and that of our people. To some extent within the perspective of our Christian belief we acknowledged our new circumstances as going through a spiritual battle field in the spiritual realm as we waded through the system rewriting our family history. It was a situation that made our senses piqued towards local fashion and materialistic consumption trends and choices. It was as if we noticed how people started to flaunt their lifestyle before us. How they looked down at us knowing that we were struggling. As a family we all went into our own pits of Humility trying to get out of this cycle of financial shortage trying to drown us.

We became more convinced than ever that it was not normal. In fact, it was evil at its worse state. Here we were so busy trying to put food on the table as the grass grew on the lawn and the weeds wind spent and dusty became scraggly foot paths on our door steps. The clothes on our backs became rags. Doors began to shut from us. It was like death spell was unleashed on us. It devoured every goodness from within our family.

I remember Tambu Tina's tale of their family woes. How the person who had put the evil eye had watched them tentatively every day to see the power of the evil spell he had cast upon them. How they had prayed and tried to find what ailed them and after much prayer a house healer had visited the house and told them that the person had put something under the stairs of the house. Such that in the evening they would hear the toads grunting and moving about in the house.

There was a family friend and a neighbour who visit every day to see and hear what was happening in the family. This kind of behaviour seems like Tamana Gelu's attitude of coming to rake beside the house every few hours of the day. He was always on our back trying to discover what we were up to. Like an irritable itch that never went away he hovered over our very presence like a stinking scent of humanity rotting before our face.

Recriminations start to gnaw at our consciousness the cruel unfairness in life that is thrown back our face. We are struggling to survive and these so called "wannabes" in our neighbourhood are on a 'high' buying cell phone gadgets and string cutters to mow their lawns. Boom box music on full blast like a little Harlem of fools in paradise cruising to insanity with jealousy. Then a bedlam of the likes that seems to say *"if we cannot be smart as you are at least we got money to be chic and high above you, up your nose"* kind of sneer.

Thank God for the moral strength to be humble and face what life throws back at us. We continue to live as always, as we are used to using the garden scythe and broom to maintain the yard. Making good use of our block, food gardens and our networks to survive. After all, a lot of people feel inferior by your brilliance and success at university and use it to intimidate our lives and in turn our life experiences with their jealous strife.

It is like being in a dark spectre with supernatural powers beyond our control. We were under spiritual attack in a battle field we were unprepared and ill equipped to handle. As I said, we were like puppets on a stage drawn into a play in whose script we could not rehearse but improvise along the way. This is our tale of Woes.

Chapter 19

Remember Those Girls?

When you were leaving remember those two girls that came over to stay with Tamana and Kina Gelu?

Remember those pigs and the maintenance they did on their house?

Well it sort of reminds me of an adage that goes like this, *"everything that glitters is not gold". As I said.*

The Gelu's made such bad allegations.

On the other hand, the four piglets they were ogling over and showing off about, two were stolen and the other two remains. Eventually, they had to make appropriate payments for the young Bali girl's removal from their home to compensate for the piglets. As for their new house building structure, much of the fly wire and ceiling fixtures of the house has deteriorated and hangs in a disarray.

Then Tamana Gelu bought a string grass cutter that he wants to use to make a bit of income for his family. However, they have used this item as a luxury wealth signal brandishing it on a fortnightly ritual of mowing their lawn. Even when the lawn had no need to be mowed.

For a time during this period of grass cutting and yard cleaning mind games we could hear Kina Gelu's excited exclamations and announcements to all her relatives that came to visit them that they had a block at Morekea and they were planting Kaukau there. They had made the arrangements with Papa Mamo, but most people in Morekea had heard what happened to Lola and most of your aunties at Morekea just detested them both. Initially they went to see Papa Dom to allocate a plot for them but Papa Dom said he and Papa Bema had allocated you kids plots in their own family land tenure boundaries. So that's how we found out about their movements. However, Pupu Kup's other children disputed their attempt to get a block at Morekea, so now they are back to square one.

In reciting this story I noticed that what Tamana and his wife Kina had failed to understand is that Kinship roles and responsibilities were taken seriously within our indigenous society. The news of their treatment of Lola affected the family decision on their land acquisition request.

Hospitality is a Christian ministry and ancient cultural practice that involves opening one's home to visitors. It is an outward act of veneration and is about good will and kindness to people who need it. Like stewardship, hospitality is about taking responsibility of one's shared values for the sake of humanity. It is a Godly act and those who provide hospitality to others do so out of generosity and to extend God's love to humanity.

Therefore, the question that seems to emanate from this tale is how much do we love God enough to open our homes to others.

I am scribbling these as I have just found their existence today and think they ought to be part of the whole collection on Kina and Tamana Gelu series.

On another extreme incident again, it was more of a brief Public Show Mama had written ...

It's midday very windy and Tamana Gelu is raking against the strong winds. Kaiymei has a rising fever and she lies on my legs as I cradle her and write.

Roof tops clatter as tree branches swing and sway whilst their leaves rustle and howl in the wrestling tirade outside. Dust, grit and smog cover the air and we seek refuge in your room. Yet the strong winds continue to hurl dust into the windows and Kaiymei groans and moans in pain. Although, I have given her antibiotics the fever has not broken. There is no one to watch over her so I can go buy her Panadol and the feeling of hopelessness just adds to the many bad experiences I have had since yesterday.

As I am writing this I remember Kina Gelu calling from the road to her husband so the whole community can hear that she told Niko to call Dokta Meri already.

She is dressed to the nines as usual. Wanting the neighbourhood to notice her Missus Kilos outfit. Her high heels grate the elephant grass on the bushy bush track. Her hair pulled back in a neat bun emphasizes her protruding forehead like the lead bumper of the latest Ford land cruiser at Ela Motors car sales depot display; but she is determined to be the razor mama for the village settlement so we all watch the show with much laughter in our midst.

Her children look at her with embarrassed annoyance and wait for her to depart before they leave the house.

Chapter 20

Violent Stance In The Game

Do you remember Papa's work friend Uncle James?

Just before Easter he had succumbed to diabetes when he refused to amputate his leg to save his life. He was eventually buried in his family block in Hoskins. Poor Papa sat so silent in grief for his friend.

We have been experiencing those strong violent winds again in the past few weeks. The difference now is that it has gone far longer than it normally does, too long. These forces of nature seem to have been stirred up from an aggressive dreamscape that has spilt into our reality, our world. Old people who read the natural phenomena say someone must have opened up Pandora's box and the forces of evil run amok on human nature as the battle of good and evil starts to play out in our landscape.

Or artificial intelligence robot spouses are creating a world of anxiety. Whatever the reason, the aggression of its ongoing attitude of hurling a torrent of gusts and grits to no end around us like a scorned lover, has since become unbearable. There is barely any defense, none, against these natural forces on us. The earth scrambles to stand in the fury of the wind as she thrashes the trees, shrubs and flowers from their stalk throwing insults aimlessly. These fleeting sparks of angry spats have affected our health and patience. Roofs of houses have been screeching and thumped every now and then. Dust bowls rise and fall intermittently all over the place while the scorching heat continues its penetrating glare.

People only venture out of their homes to complete urgent tasks. While the office workers and school students take off early in the morning dawn when the morning mists start to disperse in the new day's fast spreading rays. We are vigilantly watching that buai tree next to the kitchen because it's half rotten and may fall on our house. Papa as usual has delayed the tasks on the excuse of no rope to direct the tree's fall. However, Tamana Gelu who has the means and ropes at his disposal makes no moves to assist Papa resolve this imminent threat.

He has been as sneaky as the devil's advocate and ally, watching from a distance, grumbling and mumbling at me and my actions. His flowers all died because he planted them on a swamp area and waters them at midday during his lunch break.

Now he's doing window dressing with the ginger lilacs. Papa says he probably comes from the city and never planted anything in his entire lifetime. To me he seems to be mocking God all the time by his actions. His actions can loudly be heard as, *"look at me I can plant flowers too. Look at my house. Look at me cleaning my house."* One time Kina spoke out loud ,"*Look at them they can walk over unswept paths.*" The more they speak about their plans, they become thwarted and they are as belligerent as ever.

The winds have thwarted his intentions so the big act of raking leaves has stopped. Now his flowers, wind swept and blown, are replaced by very mature lilacs. It is as if all that they had crafted has crumpled up in front of their faces so that now they cannot see to what end the wrapper has come undone. He has lost the plot of his play and replaced the dead with the living dead in his window. The front of his yard tells of his strive to mimic others and the plant he has planted is the one that is called the deceiver.

Now the winds have come his house's flywire has all gone. The roof screeches and threatens to fly off. Whilst, the ceiling has collapsed with all its trimmings. Their house structure and frame resembles a chicken coop all painted up nicely from the outside. That is how he and his wife have created an image of their marriage and family life for all to see. They pretend to be somebody and something they are not. How they fall with broken pride as if their wings are clipped.

After my role playing outbursts over the phone episodes they stopped showing off with their mobile phones. One time Kina Gelu said that she could have gone to university but she got married.

The saying "*Jealous nogat marasin*" has since become her personal affliction. In all these public rants by Kina Gelu, Tamana Gelu is a symbol of a long-suffering husband.

She dresses to the nines with suit and high heels as a teacher's assistant at the settlement outside of town and looks down at people. An attitude which Papa commented wryly as an afterthought that m*aybe she doesn't know any decent office job except being a teacher.* Now that I have come to give it some thought, there might be some truth in this statement.

Chapter 21

Minding My Own Business

I have been sewing Kaiymei's hair bands, dresses blouses, bags and maintaining my braids so Kina Gelu, has been itching for an argument. In my head I'm thinking how dumb she is trying to compete with a *gareh** (an old woman) like me.

She has lost her marbles already, I think. Phew!

Sigh!

I do my eye rolls as I continue my chores.

She thinks it's chic to smoke tobacco rolled on scraps of newspapers. Taking long drags in the front yard she calls to by standers so they can see her. Pretending to act like the office women she puts on a show trying to get the public.

Apparently, all their plans for the year have all been unsuccessful. That reminds me, have I mentioned also that they had since sold off their Block at Nivani?

Lately, they have planted a small plot of a soup garden at the end of their back yard in Bata Lincoln's Cocoa block. That is a little testy situation with this arrangement though, with regards to informing and seeking Pupu Lo'oh's consent. They often seemed not aware how traditional land tenure systems are concerned just like Back Page and all her shameful empty words of vanity.

On that note, this is how they have brought on Back Page into the whole framework of family political rivalry. They have built on alliances in our family politics that eventuated upon new development of Back Page's family life situation.

Soon after you left it had become apparent to everyone that Back Page and her husband had sold off all their residence land titles at town peles under the pressure of Rambo's father, lapun Suitim Nus. She has move to nambis peles building a permanent house next to aunty Vivi and Sisi man.

Her move there has been aggressively violent, where she is having consistent rows with aunty Vivi for various reasons. All these dramas took place whilst Papa Rex, the custodian of the land area, went to Kaliai and this is a very tense situation because aunty Vera opposed Back Page building her house.

Apparently, Dido overhead a conversation Tamana and Kina Gelu had with Back Page regarding their interest in building a flat under Back Page's house. So now they have forged a close working alliance with each other to settle at nambis peles.

The irony in all this is that Papa Gee, Papa Rex and many others in the family and the extended community want Papa to go to nambis peles and evacuate them. Papa is reserved in this matter because he says Papa Gee is living outside in that hamlet, not him, so as the immediate elder, he has to resolve the matter. Before I forget I must mention here that I have since come to see her Kina Gelu as the devil incarnation of Jezebel.

In recent weeks we have had a message sent to us to deliberate on our water front blocks. The people who had asked to have the meeting had no authority to make the decision. This is derived from a younger brother who neither contributes to our family gatherings and has never given birth to a child trying to make decisions on our children's block.

Thank fully, no one attended and Sisi man's word to them is to not to have discussion on the blocks. By virtue of customary rights we have already acquired those rights and therefore she and others seeking these intervention plans had no authority to issue orders.

As clearly disguised, we later came to find out that Tamana and Kina Gelu were part of this purported plot to discuss our water front blocks. This has added some reflective insight to this move within the family to access our surplus blocks. Our angels were busily at work protecting us from the evil intents of those plotting against us making us realise that we indeed serve a living spirit.

Ha! But do you remember the jinxed part that I was concerned about?

Well soon after the Wok Kastom, two days later to be precise Kina Gelu fell mysteriously ill. Tamana Gelu escorted her to the hospital for treatment. For three days her body was harangued and wasted into a skeletal frame. It would take at least a week for her body to heal.

It was around that time I received my first full paying client for my writing services company that I had registered. It was like waking up in a cocoon after a long sleep when I walked into the Provincial government offices again. Most senior officers had retired or passed on whilst a new generation, much younger, were in the refurbished offices. Everything had changed so much in a short space of time.

I had a list of business contacts that I used until Papa got healed. Somehow our life was all starting to be revived again. During the whole week I went to places that I would never have thought of but because the job had to be done I got cleaned up and attended to the tasks. Whilst, Papa babysat Kaiymei.

It was at this time that I realised a change in Kina and Tamana's behaviour at home. They had so suddenly gone quiet. Sometimes I would notice both of them just sitting there hiding themselves away inside their house listening and whispering softly behind their closed doors.

An odd sort of suspicion crept into my mind thereafter like the question of whether they plotted to jinx us at the recent Wok Kastom? Given their enthusiasm for wanting to know whether we were attending or not. Their shock and disappointment that we did not but had been given some recognition. They had arrived back disappointed at the results of their efforts going unrecognised.

They were particularly angry that we had not attended the event in person as well. This is because we noticed how miserable and disappointed they had become after the event; o f t e n at times we would hear them groaning out aloud at our conversations. Tamana Gelu's raking temporarily ceased as he groaned and whispered in their room.

Even despite the fact that we had very little in our pockets and in the kitchen, we continued to reach out to the many people who sought out our assistance. Money was not the secret of our success but respect. We have values that guide our behaviours and standards in life that extends our life long relationship with others. These are cultured essences that proud self-conceited persons will find it hard to emulate.

That week and most especially on the day of the Wok Kastom of *Pahapipit,* Kina Gelu was on her toes and every now and then they spoke out aloud to get people's attention. By late afternoon she came back empty handed but rowdier than ever because Hegu's parents asked them to arrange for her police man relative to come in the morning and put down the pig, Tawaki for the kastom Wok.

On the morning of the day of the Wok Kastom the couple diligently completed their tasks. After that, Kina Gelu sat all day there with Back Page and your Sisi man at the main arena. Papa Leo ignored them for the Mapah distribution and the things on the poda disappeared before their eyes. They all came back empty handed except Papa who got the highest mapah in the family of tupla ten.

During the day after Tamana Gelu delivered the pig he returned home and started raking his yard and asked Papa whether he would be attending the Wok Kastom. Papa said that he had nothing to contribute so he won't be attending. So Tamana asked again whether I was at the Wok Kastom and Papa replied that 1 was in the house doing some paper work. To which he had nothing to add because it was unusual for us to miss a family Wok Kastom.

Just as I had feared people had expected us to be at this Wok Kastom and had we been there something would have happened to either one of us. Around about three o'clock in the afternoon, as Papa stood on the front veranda, he noticed the people coming back from the Wok Kastom. In the first group Watermelon and her children walked in quiet cheerful strides while at a long distance behind them B.G, Kina Gelu and Back Page walked with icy silence.

By then Papa mentioned out aloud for me to hear that the Wok Kastom had not been favourable to many people. It was at that time after that solemn crowd passed that little Pedro brought over tupla ten pram tambu letting Papa know that there were no coins added to it.

We were very happy in this mapah and for the way we had contributed to the Wok Kastom. Papa Gee and Papa Jim, Hegu's father, had received the highest Mapa on the occasion.

The day after the Wok Kastom Kina Gelu was in her worst mood mumbling complaints to Tamana Gelu about the outcome of the mapah distribution. However, as far as Papa and I recalled when the deceased was alive none of our family members ever visited her or interacted with her. During the funeral too they did not take an active role in the Wok Kastom rites. It is only on the day of the distribution of the mapah that they came to receive and Papa Jim gave them the cold shoulder treatment.

Papa commented that in Wok Kastom you have to be wise in how you play your role. It is not something for the faint hearted to understand. We had been wise in how we contributed, giving in the areas that were significant and at the time where it was required so it could be recorded.

This is just another snippet of Tamana and Kina Gelu.

They had seen Anna coming to get assistance from us so they started going outside to find out how we were assisting them. Later Jay was coming so they started keeping tabs on Jay from Feli.

Whew! Ha, that Tamana Gelu. He is like a sticky beak old woman putting his nose into people's business wanting to know about you, Feli and Hegu's life. He better be careful because Kirap sek, his own daughter, might give him grief for teasing his brothers daughters. Life is a very unpredictable thing. He is a very devious person with bad intentions. He has become an abomination to his own people in marrying that woman, Kina Gelu.

Papa and I have grown old looking at the world and living the drama it brings to us. Now our ages go even further as our body starts to shrink but we learn to look past those trivial titbits, but for Tamana and Kina, who have become the snidest jokes towards us, they are an example of the worst-case scenario of *"Jealous nogat marasin "*.

It is my hope in you reading this is that you will go on and complete that degree so that your sister Jay, Papa and Mama in New camp as well as us can at least release our breath in full.

I don't know what got into Dido today but he said, *"Tamana Gelu bai luk stret taim Annie graduate na holiday wok.Bai mi bai lukim ol. Boi mas pilim lon bun na stap"*. (He got so emotional about something).

Kina Gelu and Tamana are trying to support Back Page to build their house on Pupu man's area so they will put their house rent there. They are ganging up outside and told Pupu No'oh they applied for a loan to use. These days they are singing and teasing, yelling out to me that I am jealous of them as they are big shots.

This puts off Dido and he doesn't like to stick around the area. Whilst, Kaiymei has started to talk clearly now. Too much complaining that food doesn't taste alright to the point when she complains that we are greedy if we do not feed her. She complains too about wanting to chew betelnut. She has become a little chatter box.

We have been experiencing those strong violent winds again in the past few weeks. The difference now is that it has gone far too long then it normally does. These forces of nature seemed to have stirred up from an aggressive dreamscape that has spilt into our reality, our world.

Old people who read the natural phenomena say someone must have opened up Pandora's box and the forces of evil run amok on human nature as the battle of good and evil starts to play out in our landscape.

Then there are folks who say that nature could be upset by some turn of events. The political deals on the intrusion, violation and raping of our natural environment is as unprecedented as ever in our human history. The deal to dump nuclear waste on our shores, sea bed mining activities and artificial intelligence robot spouses are creating a world of anxiety.

Whatever the reason, the aggression of its ongoing attitude, hurling gusts and grits with no end around us like a scorned lover has since become unbearable. The wind storms represent Tamana and Kina, when they are a iconoclastic symbol of idiosyncratic values when they pretend to be something that they are not.

Chapter 22

After The Wind storm

In this particular day, in the early hours Back Page came to harass us, there was a light drizzle of rain drops. It was the beginning of four long days of cold nights and rainy days when the lawns started to look nourished again. The showers wiped away the volcanic dust and the air got clean once more. It was like the beginning of something new, a renewal of faith and hope in times of grave challenges and trials of human hardship in the face of adversity.

It sort of represented a contradiction of convictions. An awakening of sorts in our midst. It was also the time I found out about the new saint for young people Blessed Carlo Atticus, a Mexican soon to be sainted for Young people and Computer Technology. Some Catholic friends of mine say he is a very powerful saint when it comes to computer technology and internet issues so I thought I might mention him to you.

After Back Page had come and did the rampage, Tamana and Kina Gelu had a hard time of trying to stay at home because we were not talking and trying to resolve the issues as we sorted out our administration. By Tuesday in the heavy down pour we heard Tamana

Gelu raking again whistling and teasing and trying to intimidate us.

It is at times like this that I always try to understand why God would allow psychopaths on our path when we are giving the best we can in our community projects and living the best way we can by honouring Him.

The Gelus are like hound dogs in our neighbourhood drooling into our property with their hang dog curiosity. His description is more like the darker shade of man in our midst with his own mental issues. An unreliable character, a public figure who needs to be reminded of the tentative consequences of breaking the Christian commandment of thou shall not covet what is not yours. Also the fact that they cannot hold some sort of leadership role in public is also getting to him.

He moves with trepidation, since the land incident, trying to pick up the momentum again of intimidating us. We have been praying for shields and cover, but it is you and Dido who are making the situation spiral out of control by not obeying us in the instructions we kindly ask you to follow or obey. One of which is to refrain from communicating with Back Page and her son. On Wednesday Papa replanted and cleaned the taro garden. He also cleaned the small patch that aunty Flo had allotted to us to plant some aibika. Tamana Gelu sat watching singing and teasing as he watched Papa. They had assumed that we had accumulated loss but it seemed as if we had risen above that rampage clearing up the debris replanting and starting up the new garden again. They are at it again.

Dad went to the block yesterday around midday so Kina and Tamana were at their worst selves again given Dido's absence. They always wait for you guys to leave and they will attack me using their psychological intimidation, more like the devil's play ground where their emotions run haywire in front of me. I guess I am one of those spiritual people that has the spiritual ability to discern the evil intents of those who wish ill harm on me.

Even Kaiymei now can discern their attitude so sometimes I notice that she would try to distract me when they are jeering to chat with me or make little playful games. Kaiymei has also grown up in her cognitive interactions. Like I mentioned in another story that her very presence epitomises religious intellectual humility in resilience to her own personal situation.

Trying to make themselves look important and teasing me in the process, Kina and Tamana start the day's nuisances. At midday after much discussion Tamana leaves for their block and Kina wears this "sagana" length shorts and "bros" tight t-shirt (me, eye rolls and shaking my head) and sits under the house with some papers and pretends to be busy.

I am busy with my new phone editing my draft proposal on the living room bed when I notice Kaiymei is shivering. Her limbs are covered in goose bumps as she swings her upper limbs to and fro on the bed in rapid motions, trying to shake off the fever. Upon checking her body warmth I cover her up with a warm blanket and give her pain killer pills to contain the fever before carrying her to your room because it's cooler than the living room where splashes of hot air and the sun blazes in. There inside your room we both doze off until after four in the afternoon when I wake up.

By then the sun had made a long descent from the sky making the place cooler all around. Feeling nauseated and bloated I make my way outside to sit on the verandah to cool off.

After I had recovered, I decided to get Kaiymei out of the room to the living room to feel the clean air because I suspected the room was sending bad vibes making both of us sicker than we were. After I placed her down on her bed Kaiymei wakes up and I feed her with a fresh boiled egg. With exposure to clean air in the living room she is revived but neither talks or converses with me so I am at a dilemma how to get dinner started and at the same time monitor her condition.

While I am pondering behind the curtains I hear Kina rising from her silent presence back into her jeering and snide comments, out loud, and adding sarcasm to her words of folly. I am still sitting next to Kaiymei when I detect the change in both the volume and tone of Kina's voice. It is then I also hear Tamana's voice. I peek through the windows to see the commotion and see that it was one of those rare moments when Tamana seems lost and unable to respond to Kina's verbal deluge. He is just standing there in front of the house at the water pump facing his wife looking aloof and helpless from her tirades.

In a marathon record time before us, Kina has changed her attire slipping on a meri blouse over her tee shirt and wrapped a lavalava on her shorts before starting to walk out of their yard. A hand bag has mysteriously appeared, strewn carelessly over her shoulders as her voice becomes hoarse in bursts of obscenities and threats flying off into the empty air space as she half walks and runs towards Tangana line. In between the snatches of their conversation, I get a grip of what has transpired. One of their tenants had taken a court order on them for them to appear before one of the village pop up clans land group over their Block at Nivani. Kina is belligerent that they could dare to take action against them. Both the tenant and the pop up clan land group. group.

Empathy is something I find hard to feel for them and feel the urge to say *"serves them right"* for all the misery they have meted out to me but I refrain and bear it all inside. I feel like a martyr already for all the trouble they put me through. Tamana and Kina Gelu have become the greater folly of our neighbourhood trying to belittle their elders like me.

After they had returned home by night fall, they took all their children and went to see Pupu man for his counsel. Around mid-night they returned home. We had forgotten about Kaiymei's affliction and given kopiko to her resulting in her not being able to sleep till two o'clock in the morning. That's how we heard their arrival. Kaiymei blasted the radio station on dad's phone and danced till late annoying both Kina and Tamana Gelu who groaned loudly intermittently in the dark; much to our chagrin may I add.

On an afterthought, I believe that God took care of them for me but they are so into themselves to realise all these tribulations they face.

Yesterday I went to our legion meeting again. I was very late. Last week they held the prayer meeting one day earlier so they could attend Pupu Voga's Wok Kastom. Dad told me of the change of schedule so I missed last week's meeting. The Saturday morning and apostolic pastoral visits in the community are done on Tuesday and Thursdays. I am thinking of going for the apostolic wok prayer meetings because they are only eight members in Ruango Catholic Parish Community (CPC).

Papa in, his most know it all solemn tone, has commented rather wryly that, *"hevi bai hitim femli blo yu stret sapos yu join. Bikpla traim save bungim ol lain like mekim wok blo sios tingting gut na go."*

His premonition of caution over my intending involvement has filled me with anxiety and trepidation on my decision. My mind vexes in between the pros and cons of joining this ministry. A little voice has been persistently reminding me that the life we live now is already hard given the threat in premonitions by Papa to me. It convinced me to stand up and look closely all around the neighbourhood because there are people around us God has blessed with all the good things of this world who should be the ones to join legion not me. Given the ongoing challenges I continue to face in my life it would seem madly insane for me to serve a God who relishes my suffering yet expects me to begrudgingly continue to strive to please him. In the darkness of my poverty-stricken state I ask myself repeatedly, "what good purpose would it serve" and also "a fool it is to become martyr in my dire poverty stricken state"? It is as if the analogy, where a battered wife would go back to the mad man who has already chopped her hand off in the first place.

In writing these stories to you they become a journal of coping with life since you left. It paints a poignant picture of what the African American novelist, Toni Morrison said in her novel "Jazz" in the following statement "I lived a long time, maybe too much, in my own mind". She goes on to say that "I agree with what others have been saying about me but if you have been left standing as I have been would you have felt the same way as I have?" Is it the same way with you?

They started to murmur in soft voices, walking with quiet bowed heads pretending to be somewhere else than there. They knew they were guilty by association and did not know how they would be allies with people here so they were sneaking off, and much to their seething rage the boys were watching.

There was a Wok Kastom for Marvin's mother at town ples so Dido went and kori to Bart Papa Toff's son. He received his share and Papa received pram tambu from Wano and his brother Nick. Like at Morekea, Papa and I did not go but we received something. Also not all family members received *pram tambu mapah*. As usual Back Page was one of those who missed out and was livid with the outcome.

At after midnight, in a drunken stupor, Back Page came and tried to attack Papa. Papa ignored her and came in the house. As usual she screamed and put on a tantrum and went away.

She came back after one o'clock in the early hours of the morning but we almost slept through it, her huffing, puffing and snivelling like a pig around the house. Getting all worked up swearing and calling Papa obscenities she raved on and on like a mad person. Sometimes she gave him death threats saying that her son would murder Papa.

We prayed inside and ignored her. She left but not before destroying our taro garden and everything in it. Telling Papa useless "Brudee", with their falling apart match box house in between swearing insults. It was all so evil we just felt so tired and ignored her. We heard Tamana and Kina Gelu assisted them. In the morning Papa informed Pupu No'oh who got photos of the damage and made a police statement of the incident to make her pay damages.

Later Papa and Dido took everything she uprooted and went and deposited it on her front steps. Sisi man was so embarrassed he ran away when he saw what both of them did. When people met them on the way there they both told the people that a pig destroyed our food garden so they are bringing the stuff to the owner's house.

I told off Tamana and Kina Gelu: "*Lukim size blo Annie and Andrew no one will scare me off or force me off my block. I will plant and decorate my house, yard and live here as long as I am alive. People who think like idiots with a jealous mindset that will water plants on a swampy soil at midday when the sun is hot. These are the very people who destroyed my garden. Sorry tough luck, jealous nogat marasin, I will plant more taros and aibika and flowers,*" I added further.

When they both heard this they took their children and left the house all day.

Dido was not with us when this incident happened. It was only after Papa was with Pupu No'oh that I went over to the haus boi and brought him over that he realised what had happened. On reflecting upon the situation, it is because she knew that Dido was at the haus boi she came and attacked Papa. Also because Dido disobeys Papa and visits her, she thinks that she can attack Papa in front of Dido and Dido would not even lift a finger to stop her. This is what happened that night.

Dido told us later that she called out to him as she was coming to the house, that she and her son will murder Papa sometime soon. She did all this quietly and the boys didn't hear. Later they all heard what had happened and were upset. Most of them were keeping watch at Pupu Rick's place as he had suffered a stroke soon after the peace ceremony. Although, there were some boys in the area everyone was in their own yard alert to any disturbances that might occur.

Dido mentioned that the reason why Back Page was under great pressure was because the time to compensate Papa blo baby's baby was due the following weekend. As were his other crime related demands including the one at New camp. She was feeling the ping of people's angst towards her over her son's crimes. Nowadays, many people did not respect her and were ignoring her, causing her grief. She was therefore releasing her frustration at Papa for this pent-up anger.

Every time, she comes to complain about our lifestyle, throwing obscenities and threats at us when we have no issues with her. We don't want to know her or have anything to do with her. She harasses us and destroys our property and goes around spreading rumours about us.

What came out of her mouth that night was what was previously in Kina Gelu's mouth. The raving insecurities of our demise as if she had a perfect life. She is a mad woman "*hooliwonga*".

Her words and actions were complementary to Tamana and Kina Gelu as were Watermelon's, Mista and Missus Missionary who constantly gripe at us over their consumption wealth.

Like the ancient drama of the Greek Civilisation our lives revolve over tragedy, one after another. Time passes as drama evolves making our lives richer through the emotions they trigger. In them we witness the characters of human beings under duress. Stretching and meandering along the paths of decisions they choose. In our back water of the Pacific, we experience those stirrings of Awakening and social drama too.

Here in our village, life is never dull where women cry over perceived wrongs and men are shrewd landowners of their land. While the young ride over the emotional intensity of flaming lives and lost loves.

Our stories have gone into our place of 'special place' memories, but the intrusion of outsiders and their cultures dominate and dictate our version of looking at life through *their* lens. It is how this next story evolves. The trials and drama of angst.

There was a brief interlude after the rain storm of four days. Now it is the fifth day and the sun is back as fierce as ever scorching the earth with her glares. She has stirred the belly of the winds as they start to swish past the trees over the air, searching and looking for God knows what.

We have started to put the wet laundry out on the lines outside to dry. Papa moved the bamboo stalls in the front yard as he trims the lawn.

Somehow the brief interlude was a recuperating time for us to look at the big picture and move on to our track again.

I am waiting for Jay to come sign the state declaration form so I can send it off, so I do some outstanding administrative work in the house as Papa also does outstanding chores around the house. Now that I have come to think long about it, somehow Back Page and her son remind me of the Greek tragedy Electra. Whilst, this latest development has got Papa really sick it is you and Dido not taking your studies seriously and that is provoking opportunists to attack him.

Back Page now has gone to Kedo Wakapi, planting a new garden and a row of new coconut trees on their side of the garden. She goes to our block with her husband provoking Papa, Back Page says, "*who cares about Papa, her son will take over all of Papa's block. Ol pikinini blo yu bai mekim wanem?*". She jeers at Papa these days.

She knows that our only means of income is copra and it is only Papa that does this work. Dido doesn't like to go to the block on his own neither does he babysit Kaiymei, so I too am hopeless to assist Papa. That is why we are struggling and not getting enough to send to you any allowances on a consistent basis. Even our enemies like the Gelus, Missus Missionary and Watermelon see these difficulties and take advantage of our vulnerabilities. Like the drama of ancient civilisation these latest dramas of the local people in our village are interesting morals from which to learn despite the spite they bring into our lives.

Tamana Gelu and his wife are like little children steeped in the lust of coveting, craving to emulate our lives. Never living theirs but trying to chase us through their greed. Their evil intent visible and naked as the scorching sun that beats the barren soil of the plain playing fields in our school yards.

Whilst, Missus Missionary's proud nose looks down on her neighbours like the stuck-up middle class she esteems to be but cannot reach by her snobbery.

Whilst, Watermelon takes the crutches of ignorance to assert her biases over others. Why should I be this less when you are just as I am? She seems to be portraying in her actions. Back Page and her son are like Electra and her son, whose incestuous affairs and family tragedy ended an empire.

Ha! Well, that's life then.

End

Acknowledgements

I feel that our stories can be read without judgemental notes on our heritage and condescending comments on our status as writers, story tellers and keepers of our people's voices. It truly has been a long journey of acceptance for me as writer to come to this level of completing this project. So, Thank you.

There are lots of people who deserve to be mentioned and acknowledged but I want to thank my extended family in Ruango village especially. Mr and Mrs Rubenet for sponsorship of electricity and moral support to my family, our village elders and family members in Kawutu Wakore and Tangana Pogi who assisted me on numerous occasions in various ways. In a similar instance I want to thank and acknowledge my children Lebo Koi, Taroa and Waiyora Kondi as well as my loving husband Lolote who has remained my constant support team in all my life.

I also acknowledge my mother Annlyn Mota who had been the first story teller in my life. Despite her busy schedule as a working mum she had always found time to tell stories from her heritage. It was from her that I first heard the traditional Kiki Agata Bamba stories from the Korafe Mokorua language. Through her she taught me Kaita poetry in its many verses. My paternal grandmother Madeleine Kitako was a traditional poet who composed the Gasegha poetry in its many variations but it was my father's aunt, my namesake Avia Constance Yariba who taught me about little ways of reading nature. My aunties Kaiymei and Imuyah were my companions sorting through the dreams the signs and reading symbols of how our people explained our living spaces evolving challenges. When I got married and moved to Ruango the women elders at Ruango and Morekea villages patiently passed on traditional notes of living in their traditional society which formed the basis of the cultural materials in this book.

I would also like to thank my support networks through my various social media platforms over the years who have exchanged ideas and discussed some aspects of this project in their respective cultural themes.

www.ingramcontent.com/pod-product-compliance
Lightning Source LLC
Chambersburg PA
CBHW020516120726

47904CB00003B/855